DEATH SPINS THE WHEEL

AN INSPECTOR LITTLEJOHN MYSTERY

GEORGE BELLAIRS

AGORA BOOKS

ABOUT THE AUTHOR

George Bellairs was the pseudonym of Harold Blundell (1902-1982). He was, by day, a Manchester bank manager with close connections to the University of Manchester. He is often referred to as the English Simenon, as his detective stories combine wicked crimes and classic police procedurals, set in quaint villages.

He was born in Lancashire and married Gladys Mabel Roberts in 1930. He was a devoted Francophile and travelled there frequently, writing for English newspapers and magazines and weaving French towns into his fiction.

Bellairs' first mystery, Littlejohn on Leave (1941), introduced his series detective, Detective Inspector Thomas Littlejohn. Full of scandal and intrigue, the series peeks inside small towns in the mid twentieth century and Littlejohn is injected with humour, intelligence and compassion.

He died on the Isle of Man in April 1982 just before his eightieth birthday.

DEATH SPINS THE WHEEL

GEORGE BELLAIRS

1

EBB TIDE

When news of the violent death of Madame Garnier reached Ronaldsway Airport, P.C. Pallister of the airport squad was seized with unusual fury and broke into language that his father, a Methodist elder, would have reproved.

'I wish I could lay me hands on the bloody swine that did it!'

The nice old girl, he had called her, although they had met and parted all in the space of a few minutes. Now she had been murdered. It seemed to P.C. Pallister the limit in cruelty and waste.

On Thursday, July 2nd, the old lady had stepped from the incoming plane from London and made straight for P.C. Pallister.

'I understand there is a hotel at the casino here, officer. Can you recommend it and how do I get to it?'

A small old lady, thin, pink-cheeked, white haired and immaculately dressed in a smart light costume. She spoke good English but you could tell from the intonation and the careful way she picked out her words that she was a foreigner.

Pallister had wondered whatever in the world had brought her, all alone, to the Isle of Man. She had quite captivated him. She was vivacious and gracious and it was difficult not to believe that she was a younger actress playing the part of an elderly aristocrat.

The constable had taken her in hand, although he'd pretty soon gathered that she could look very well after herself. He'd mustered her three pieces of expensive luggage, whistled up a taxi, and sent her on her way full of information.

'Is it a good casino, officer?'

Pallister had never crossed the threshold of the place. His dad had vigorously opposed the new law legalising gambling and the establishment of a centre in which to indulge in it. Even if P.C. Pallister *had* been in the casino. He had no standards by which to measure its efficiency and adequacy. All the same, anything Manx was good to Pallister.

'Quite good, ma'am. It has an excellent reputation.'

And then she'd bidden him good-bye and given him a pound note. Pallister hoped that neither his dad nor his sergeant heard of this encounter.

That was the last he saw of Madame Garnier alive.

The taxi deposited her at the door of the hotel at noon. They gave her the best room in the place after she'd registered.

Mme Garnier,
Bel-air,
Evian-les-Bains.

The hall porter dealt with her luggage.

'First thing she asked was where's the casino. Behind that red curtain, I told her. She didn't seem to be very impressed some-how,' he later told the police. 'She went and saw her room and was back right away and into the gaming-rooms.'

The man who collected the cash and issued the membership tickets for the casino also had a word to say about her. He was usually known familiarly as 'the chap on the door', but madame had addressed him as *régisseur*. He liked that.

It sounded good. Like Monte Carlo. He was on her side from the beginning.

The *régisseur* had dug out madame's application form for membership. He waved it about like a banner.

'She was a bit of a caution. She seemed to find the form very amusing. When she'd written out her full name, I thought she was having a bit of a joke.'

He pointed it out to the detective.

Mme. Veuve Edouard Garnier de Carry-le-Rouet.

He thought that at this point he'd better educate the detective.

'Madame Veuve means, so to speak, Mrs Widow. She was the widow of Edward Garnier, you see. It's a way the French have of putting it. And the *de* means *of* and Carry-le-Rouet is where her estates are. So, you see, she must have been a bit of a nob.'

The *régisseur's* pronunciation was purely phonetic and the policeman snatched the form and read it himself in good GCE French.

'Who told you all that?'

'One of the croopeers. He once worked in France.'

'Oh.'

'When it came to filling-in her occupation, she put down "professional gambler", as you'll see. She didn't look that sort at all and I told her so. But she seemed quite serious about it. As for her age, which you'll note is also asked for on the form, she told me I'd have to guess that and not to feel in the least embarrassed about it. I said that was her business. So, she wrote down "over twenty-one". I thought I'd let it go at that.'

'How long did she take membership for?'

'Fourteen days. She said that really ought to be long enough. I didn't quite gather what she meant by that. Personally, I got the impression she was a novice having a bit of a flutter. It seems I was wrong.'

Madame Garnier had fumbled her way through the red curtains and entered the makeshift gaming-rooms. Three regency rooms of the hotel turned into a temporary casino until the real thing could be built. Old ornamental ceilings with plaster panels and medallions overlooking a motley assortment of American gambling equipment. The old lady had looked with a wry grimace at the fruit machines which scarcely left an inch to spare in the space along the walls, and made for the only roulette table operating.

Three sailors from a visiting frigate, a man in a light suit and white shoes whose blood-pressure seemed to be rising with the play, and a raddled middle-aged woman smoking a cigarette and completely immersed in the game. A couple of croupiers, pale-faced and heavy-eyed from night work, and a bored cashier with a cigarette in the corner of his mouth.

Madame took some chips and began to make straight bets on one number. Nobody gave her a second look. She seemed to be learning the game.

After a preliminary round of losses, the old lady casually took a piece of paper from her bag and started in earnest. Still nobody bothered. The officials were used to visitors with systems. Long lists of numbers in which, somehow, they thought they saw law and order.

The old lady's bets continued without complications. One or two newcomers entered and joined the play. A man in a light drill suit arrived and throughout played an accompaniment to the roulette by frenziedly operating a one-arm bandit, amassing a heap of small winnings and then grinding them back in the machine.

An hour later, Madame Garnier took out a silver cigarette case, lit a cigarette with a little gold lighter and, after the cigarette, she held the flame under her scrap of paper. When it had been reduced to ash, she ground it out in an ash tray. Then she left the room about two hundred pounds in pocket.

The man in the drill suit was still punishing the same fruit machine.

When the old lady reached her room, she fastened the door, unlocked a suitcase, opened the false bottom, put in her winnings, and took out a locked diary in which she inserted a small key from a chain round her neck. She copied a further series of numbers and symbols on a blank sheet of paper, placed it in her handbag, and re-locked the diary and suitcase. Then she went down to lunch.

That night, she was another two hundred pounds in pocket. She never seemed to push her luck or overdo her stakes. Gently did it.

The following day a special official of the casino company unobtrusively recorded the numbers of her bets at roulette. He need not have troubled himself. For once having harvested them, neither he nor any of his colleagues could make head or tail of them. Besides, that night, Madame Garnier left the casino and did not return. After winning another hundred pounds or two in the afternoon and repeating the performance in the evening, she burned her lists of numbers and signs and left the room with great composure.

It must be confessed that the casino officials and many of the frequenters of the tables were not so tranquil. The former were beginning to feel apprehensive about what was coming next when madame began to increase her stakes. They started to make enquiries about her and discuss future policy, like medical consultants who diagnose the, as yet, faint symptoms of a relentless disease in which lies a certain prognosis of destruction.

The habitués of the tables were convulsed with curiosity. Word had got around that something queer was afoot. Secret systems as elusive and fascinating as perpetual motion, and the man who broke the bank at Monte Carlo began to be discussed. During all this Madame Garnier remained aloof. Those who sought to enter into conversation with her were courteously rebuffed and only once did she show any signs of annoyance, when an impertinent and persistent reporter found it advisable to withdraw after a fluent dismissal.

On the night of her last appearance, Madame Garnier was surrounded by a large crowd craning their necks to read the scrap of paper gripped in her fingers and consulted from time to time, holding their chips poised ready to make hasty bets on the numbers she chose.

But nobody saw the paper and few were able to follow her choice, the chips of which were rapidly placed just before 'No more bets' was called.

She left the gaming-room at nine-thirty. The late-night gamblers had not yet put in an appearance, but the tables were busy with good natured amateurs. The atmosphere had not yet acquired the tenseness stimulated by the nervous late hours and the surface sophistication of the place. There were still honest laughter and high spirits about.

The 'old lady' had by now acquired something of a reputation. The air of complete mystery about her persisted. The advent of one who was rumoured to be an international gambler and yet looked like a marquise was good publicity for the enterprise, provided it did not cost the casino syndicate too much. The news was discreetly peddled around the town and on the last evening of her life Madame Garnier was a bigger attraction than the floor-show.

When the late arrivals appeared, she was drinking coffee in the lounge and reading a copy of a day-old *Le Matin,* which the *régisseur,* as madame called him, was quick to tell everybody had arrived by post from Paris that afternoon. The *régisseur* himself had never been a polite man, but now whenever he and madame passed each other, he would bow and smile. He was always present to lift the curtain, too, and admit her to the tables. Now, he felt somewhat at a loss, with madame calmly drinking coffee in the lounge and people flocking in the gaming-rooms to watch her play. He couldn't very well approach her and suggest another game or two. Instead, he left his perch by the door of the casino, assumed a busy expression, crossed the lounge on a pretended mission, and feigned astonishment at finding madame there.

'Not playing tonight, madame?'

'No. I've had enough for one day. I'm going to take a short walk in the fresh air and then go early to bed.'

He told it all to the police later, starting with their first meeting, embellishing profusely, and then ending with their final good-night.

'It was like this...'

He told it to gamblers, reporters, police, and finally anybody who would listen. In fact, he hinted that the old lady had imparted certain gambling secrets to him which he wouldn't betray for a fortune. This gave him a certain amount of temporary prestige and self-confidence and not long afterwards he left for a job in a London club.

Mme. Garnier was seen later climbing the stairs to her room on the first floor by the man in the white shoes who had been playing at the same table on the day of her arrival and who was emerging for another flutter after reinforcing his pocket-book from a hidden reserve.

'She bade me good-night. She seemed quite happy and spry. I didn't stop to speak with her. I'd other things on my mind at the time...'

Five minutes later, she descended again. She was seen by several people, a thin silk scarf round her head and a small handbag over her wrist. The *régisseur* who was busy about his business, saw her and bowed and she answered with a gesture of her hand. Then she went out into the night.

It was just past 10.30. A warm, dry night. The last of the daylight still lingered reluctantly and etched the quiet little hills behind Douglas against the darkening blue background of the sky. The flashes of the Head lighthouse rhythmically punctuated the fading light. The muffled drumming and trumpets of the dance-halls and the shouts and singing of passers-by on the promenade drowned the sounds of late traffic.

The tide was on the ebb and dragged the water over the rattling stones of the beach.

The last person to see the old lady alive was a young constable quietly patrolling the promenade. She asked him where she could find the nearest steps from the promenade to the water's edge.

'I told her and she bade me good-night and thanked me and went down towards the tide-line. I didn't see anybody on the shore nearby. Certainly nobody followed her down the steps. I watched her to see that she got safely down and kept an eye on her till she vanished in the distance. No, I didn't hear any shot or cries for help, but then there was quite a lot of noise on the prom-enade and the tide was beating the shingle...'

A man taking his dog for a last walk came upon her just after eleven o'clock. She had been shot through the head. The earth had received her kindly and she lay like somebody sleeping.

2

THE INTRUDER

Maggie Keggin, housekeeper to the Rev. Caesar Kinrade, Archdeacon of Man, flung down the newspaper angrily. 'I knew it! That Knell will be here like a bad penny any time now. There's an old woman been murdered on Douglas sands. It's always the same when the Inspector shows his face on the Island.'

She still refused, after many years, to acknowledge the promotion of Littlejohn to Superintendent. Inspector, she contended, sounded better and more respectful.

Littlejohn and his wife were staying at Grenaby again. His doctor had forbidden the Archdeacon to do any more outdoor gardening for the benefit of his health. The parson was a keen horticulturist and only after two sturdy members of his flock had volunteered to keep the lawns trimmed and the flower beds tidy and blooming had he agreed to transfer his attentions indoors. He had purchased an aluminium annexe advertised as a Solarium and ordered stocks of begonias, cyclamen, poor-man's orchids and other exotics. Then, he had prepared to set about the do-it-yourself consignment of metal and glass and erect it himself.

Maggie Keggin had written to Littlejohn by express letter.

He'll kill himself. It's worse than digging the garden.

So, Littlejohn had arranged his holidays and, being a handy man both at home and at Scotland Yard, had volunteered to cross to Grenaby and assemble the contraption.

In a pair of old flannels and with his shirt-sleeves rolled up, he was sorting out the metal and glass whilst the concrete base dried, when his bob-tailed sheep-dog, which had been watching him with puzzled interest, gave a sharp bark, plunged through the bushes and flushed a newcomer. A tall, thin, rather shy man, grinning with pleasure, his hand outstretched. Inspector Reginald Knell, of the Manx CID

Maggie Keggin had driven him out of the house!

'Go away! Take yourself off! You and your murthers! If you start the Inspector tracking down the casino criminals, he'll have to leave the conservatory job, the Venerable Archdeacon will take over, and we'll have another dead body on our hands.'

Knell had tried to pass it off jocularly.

> 'When constabulary duty's to be done,
> A policeman's lot is not a happy one.'

'Don't try to get round me by quotin' poetry. I hope the Inspector sets the dog on you when he sees you.'

Knell and Maggie Keggin were distant relatives, so sharp exchanges did not come amiss. He told her to keep her shirt on and fled before he received an answer.

Littlejohn had time to spare whilst the base of the greenhouse grew solid and after the usual greetings and hearty enquiries, began to fill his pipe. Then he waited. It was customary for Knell, when inviting him to take a busman's holiday, to skirmish apologetically around for a bit. This time, however, the preliminaries were cut short by the arrival of the Archdeacon with three deck-chairs. He eyed Knell eagerly.

'Morning, Reginald. Have you called about the casino murder?'

Interruption. Maggie Keggin with three bottles of lager beer and glasses which she placed in the wheelbarrow. She deftly removed the caps and handed bottles and glasses to the Archdeacon and Littlejohn, but withheld Knell's until he'd struck a bargain with her.

'If the Inspector solves the crime for you, it's understood that the Archdeacon goes with him. I'm not havin' Master Kinrade killin' himself erecting greenhouses while the Inspector goes off gaddin' about with you.'

Conditions were plainly stated, promises were exchanged and Knell got his beer along with the rest.

'You see, sir,' said Knell, when they were alone at last. 'You see, sir, the case seems to have foreign complications and I thought you were more experienced in such things than me.'

'Suppose we begin at the beginning, Knell. I have only read the newspapers which are very short of detail. They seem to have been fascinated that the victim appears to have been an international gambler. Mme. Garnier, wasn't it?'

Knell frowned, took off his hat, carefully laid it on the grass and lit a cigarette.

'Yes. She lived at a place called Evian, on Lake Geneva, in France. We got in touch with the French police for some details about her. She was quite a woman!'

The Archdeacon raised his eyebrows.

'And what might we infer from that, Reginald?'

'Quite a lot, sir. She was in her seventieth year, a widow. Her late husband, Edouard Garnier, died during the war. He was a professor of something... Physics, I think.'

Here, Knell took out his notebook, a red morocco bound affair with loose leaves, a Christmas present from his wife. He thumbed it over and frowned at what he saw there.

'Professor Garnier, formerly of Montpellier and Grenoble. Madame Garnier herself was a doctor of science, but gave up teaching at Montluçon when they married, which was rather a late-in-life affair. They were both in their fifties at the time. The professor was one of the pioneers of computers...'

'Ah!'

Knell paused expectantly.

'What, sir?'

'A system on the roulette tables, a professor of physics and a computer pioneer. It all sounds very interesting. Madame, I gathered from the newspapers, was practising a very successful, if rather modest system on the tables in Douglas when she met her death.'

Knell's face lit-up as though some startling discovery had been made.

'That's right! You mention her system being modest. Well, it seems she has brothers-in-law and a sister-in-law who also live at Evian. But they didn't live together. They were always quarrelling, so kept separate establishments...'

The phrase seemed to please Knell. He muttered it to himself again.

'Separate establishments.'

'Well?'

'The French police knew Madame Garnier very well. *And* her system. She'd been very tactfully warned-off the tables at Evian casino. Not that she broke the bank there, but they thought that she might do if she made up her mind.'

'Why didn't she?'

'The Evian police had a word with her sister-in-law on our behalf. Madame Garnier, it appears, had very little interest in money itself. Her late husband was the same. She often told her sister-in-law that she only wanted to earn — which means win — enough to live on. Madame Garnier never confided in her sister-in-law, an unmarried lady, who nevertheless is known as Madame Vaud. But Madame Vaud had her own theories about the matter. In her opinion the professor, who wasn't a wealthy man, left his wife a system of gambling which would keep her very well provided for, when he died. Madame Vaud, it appears, is well off and used to urge Mme. Garnier to become the same by breaking the bank now and then. This caused a lot of quarrelling and the French police say that Madame Vaud still bears her sister-in-law a grudge about it and says she would not have come to a sticky end if she had taken her advice.'

'Had Madame Vaud any theory about why Madame Garnier met her death?'

'Plenty. She talked the French police to death. One of her ideas was that the casino officials or promoters had shot her. Which is nonsense. We'd already obtained alibis from all of them and it was hardly likely they'd do it at the height of the evening's play. In any case, they were all in the casino when madame was shot on the beach. Madame Vaud also suggested that some international syndicate had been trying to get the system out of her sister-in-law and had attempted to hold her up and take it from her. She added that Mme. Garnier was the kind who just wouldn't have believed that anyone would shoot her.'

'Why?'

'She said she was very naïve. But I don't know. Her behaviour after she arrived on the Island was far from naïve. Everybody says how sophisticated she was.'

'Madame Garnier hadn't shared her system with her sister-in-law then?'

'No. I'd venture a guess that that was what all the quarrelling was about.'

'Were particulars of the system written down?'

'Yes. Mme. Garnier kept them in a locked diary hidden in the false bottom of a suitcase, which was also well locked.'

'You found the diary?'

An uneasy look crossed Knell's face.

'Yes. Mme. Garnier had the key of the diary on a chain which we found round her neck when the body was examined. We took possession of her room at the hotel and her luggage. The doorman at the casino said he was sure that Madame Garnier had a small black handbag over her wrist when she went out for her last stroll. The handbag was missing when the body was found. It may be that whoever murdered her thought she carried written details of her system about in it. As a matter of fact, the croupier at whose table she played said she worked from a small piece of paper bearing notes and figures and after every session she set fire to it and left the bits ground to dust in one of the ash trays on the roulette table. As the handbag, which must have contained the keys of her luggage, was missing, we had to get one of our experts to deal with the locks of the suitcases. There was nothing likely to help us in our enquiries in any of them, except in the false bottom of one of them. It was very well concealed but on close examination, we found it.'

The Archdeacon, impatient at Knell's leisurely way of exposition, interrupted.

'For goodness' sake, Reginald, be a little more brief and expeditious. There's no need to work up to a dramatic climax. What did you find in the hiding-place?'

Knell bared his teeth in a broad grin.

'The diary, sir.'

'Which you opened with the key you found on the dead body. Proceed.'

'Yes. It contained a mass of figures and symbols which, I imagine, only a real mathematician could follow. We have it at the police station and it's been suggested that it be sent away for expert examination. That's really why I hurried here. I would like you, Superintendent, to have a look at it before it leaves our hands. It might hold some clues hidden in it which could help us with the case. Besides, when, to avoid delay, we rang up the Evian police direct, they spoke in French...'

'Naturally, Reginald. Naturally.'

'Well, we had to ask them if we could ring again later and had to send for the French master from the High School to act as go-between. I wished we'd had Superintendent Littlejohn there at the time. He's a fluent French scholar…'

'You flatter me, Knell. All the same, if I can be of help, I'll do my best for you.'

'Thank you, sir. You'll understand that the diary itself is a bit like a hot potato. If it contains a perfect system of winning heavily at roulette, it will be an embarrassment to somebody. If any of our men happened to have any luck at the tables — not that they'd think of playing there or would have any luck — people would say we'd got the information in the course of duty and were using it illegally…'

The Venerable Archdeacon threw up his hands.

'Really, Reginald. You have a most devious and intricate way of looking at things and worrying about them. Was there anything else in the secret part of the suitcase?'

'Yes. Over a thousand pounds in one-pound notes. Presumably Madame Garnier's winnings at the local casino and elsewhere.'

'Where had she been before she arrived on the Isle of Man?'

'Deauville, in France.'

'How did you know?'

'There was a receipt for twenty-thousand francs given by a bank in Deauville for credit of Mme. Garnier's account in Evian. She must have banked her winnings wherever she went and had them sent to her account at home. There were similar receipts from a number of other places, too. All for similar sums.'

'She apparently collected a reasonably modest amount wherever she gambled and then went on to a new place. It was a good idea. It avoided fuss and publicity. Where else had she been recently?'

'Monte Carlo, Cannes, Grasse, Vichy, Trouville, Ostend…'

'And then the Isle of Man. The casino here must be gradually earning a European reputation! Had she ever been to America?'

'Not that we could see. Her passport was in her suitcase. There was no American visa on it.'

'Did you speak with the authorities at Deauville?'

'Yes. We rang the Deauville town police...'

'You haven't let the grass grow under your feet, Knell, have you?'

Knell grinned at the compliment.

'We did our best, sir. The airport police let me know when you arrived here the other day, Superintendent, and I heard that a new greenhouse had been unloaded at the Steam Packet warehouse for the Archdeacon. I put two and two together and judged that you'd come over to help Mr Kinrade to put it up...'

The Manx grapevine seemed to miss nothing!

'I didn't want to intrude if you were busy. We got on with the details and then seemed to arrive at a dead end. Even then, I hesitated. There's always a row with Maggie Keggin whenever I show my face here and I didn't...'

The Archdeacon shuffled impatiently in his chair.

'I think that will be quite enough of your feat of detection about the greenhouse, Reginald. Suppose we return to the crime in Douglas. What did you hear from Deauville?'

'Nothing much, Archdeacon. Mme. Garnier's arrival and departure were registered on the police books from the form she filled in at her hotel. The casino knew of her, too. They reported that she played quietly and won considerable sums, but nothing that gave them much cause to worry. They said she appeared to be working on a rather successful system but seemed to know when to stop. I wondered if, somehow, these stops were a compulsory part of the system. Perhaps it went so far and then sort of ground to a halt and she had to begin all over again.'

'Or else, Reginald, she wished to attract no attention and when she reached a certain stage, she just folded up her tent and went off to another casino. I would, if possible, like to see Mme. Garnier's little diary. It is a long time since I took the Tripos at Cambridge, but it included mathematics. I promise not to make unseemly use of any information I may gather from it.'

'I'll do my best to let you have a sight of it, sir.'

'Is there any other line in the enquiry you have pursued?'

'Yes. We think her room had been searched, but whoever did it was either disturbed or else missed the false bottom in her suit-case. Whenever she went out, she left her key at the desk in the hall, but on the night she died, she told the clerk as she passed that she would keep her key in her bag as she wasn't going far and would soon be back. We found the key in the door.'

'But whoever had searched the room had made a professional job of it and left no traces of his intrusion?'

'That's right, Superintendent. All was left neat and orderly. The murderer must have taken her bag and found nothing in it about the system. That meant any notes about the play must have been in madame's room. So he returned and searched there.'

'Which might indicate it could be any Tom, Dick or Harry who'd seen Mme. Garnier successfully using her system at the tables and had made up his mind to get it and share the good fortune.'

'That's what we thought.'

Littlejohn smiled.

'And where do I come in, Knell?'

'I talked it over with the Chief and he said I might ask your advice.'

'Unofficially, of course.'

'Well, sir, it's always worked well that way in the past…'

'So you wish me to look into the matter as far as you've gone and tell you what I think… Then…?'

Knell hesitated and rubbed his chin with his forefinger.

'Well, sir. Somebody will have to go to Evian. That's certain. We'll have to try and find something about Madame Garnier's background there, won't we?'

It was Littlejohn's own method and Knell had been an eager pupil. To get the background of Madame Garnier as though he'd known her all his life. Littlejohn nodded.

'And I'm to be the lucky man?'

The Archdeacon's eyes sparkled. The greenhouse was forgotten.

'When do we start?'

It was as well that the parson wished to share the trip. It would keep him out of mischief in Littlejohn's absence, prevent his taking up where Littlejohn had left off and finishing the greenhouse job.

Knell beamed with joy.

'And when the case is over, sir, I promise I'll come and help you with the greenhouse.'

'It's a deal.'

3

THE BEWILDERED CROUPIERS

When the three of them, Littlejohn, the Archdeacon and Knell, arrived in Douglas, you wouldn't have thought there had been a murder there at all. It was as though the ebb tide, which had smoothed out the sands and carried away the rubbish as the murder was being committed the night before, had also swept away all thoughts and fears of the midnight horror as well.

The sun was shining, the sea was deep blue, and strings of little pleasure boats were bobbing across the bay. The leisurely, crowded horse-trams jingled along the promenade and the sands were packed with almost-naked sunbathers and children busy at jobs of their fertile invention. Far away the smoke of the first incoming boat from the mainland was appearing over the horizon.

A couple of sea bathers were actually drying themselves on the very spot where the body of Madame Garnier had been found the night before. No sense in roping it off; the morning tide had already washed it clean and free from anything which might be regarded as a clue or a key to the mystery.

They called at the police station, where Knell produced a medical report for Littlejohn.

'They've done the job quickly, Knell.'

Knell bared his large teeth with pleasure, almost like a horse after the taste of sugar.

'We don't let the grass grow under our feet, sir.'

Madame Garnier had been shot at close range, but from a distance which seemed to put suicide quite out of the question. The weapon itself was missing, but it had evidently been a small calibre revolver of comparatively small power. The bullet had entered the left temple and passed through the skull. The angle of the wound seemed to indicate that the murderer had been considerably taller than the victim. The brief notes of the police surgeon were subject to a check by ballistic experts. The main points were that death had been immediate and not self-inflicted.

'Would you like to see the body?'

The body! In most murders, the problem of the crime seems to crystallise apart from the flesh and blood of the victim. It was so in this case. There was a photograph of the naked corpse in the file and the surgeon's description of it. Nothing extraordinary. Already Littlejohn had built-up in his mind how Madame Garnier had looked and moved on her last night alive. Here, too, was a flash photograph of her, sprawling, face downwards on the sand, her head across her right arm, like someone asleep…

'We won't trouble you about the body. According to the doctor's report, there are no outstanding distinguishing marks, not even an operation scar. If between now and the burial, we need a sight of the body, we'll view it then.'

'You've not been to the casino since it opened last year?'

'No.'

'Care to go?'

The Archdeacon had been vigorously among the anti-casino party of the days when the idea was first mooted, but eagerly agreed to join the excursion by way of a crime investigation.

'Better the devil you know than the one you don't know. I'm really surprised at myself for not investigating the place before.'

Mme. Garnier's room at the hotel was the only one officially sealed. The gaming-rooms were open. In fact, the news of the murder had given them a shot in the arm. Usually they were deserted in the day-time. Now, however, they were as popular as the sideshows down the street and on the fairground. The roulette tables themselves were almost out of business, but the fruit machines were doing a roaring trade. You couldn't hear yourself speak for the rattle of one-arm bandits. Unlike the tables, the bandits allowed of divided attention; part for the bandit and part for the thrilling source of the murder. The attendant, who in a white coat usually patrolled the machines and stimulated the players by announcing the amounts of the jackpots to be won, had now other interests in his quiver.

'Yes. That's the table the murdered woman played at. Care to take a turn, just to be able to say when you get back home that you've played at the same wheel? No. She didn't break the bank. She knew when to stop. Just nice and steady... You should have a go...'

When Littlejohn entered the room, the one-arm bandits grew silent one by one. The players stood like statues waiting for the latest official move and people gaming in the adjoining rooms seemed to sense that something special was afoot and silently appeared, like hunters stalking prey.

'What's the bishop doin' here?' asked one of them, who'd had a few drinks and had spotted the Archdeacon's gaiters. 'Has he come to bless the roulette wheels...?'

A courteous casino supervisor showed them round. Nothing fresh came forth, nothing beyond the information given in Knell's very competent initial report. The main thing seemed to be that Madame Garnier had been a complete stranger. She hadn't known a soul there. She just came and went, played a little, won comparatively quite a nice sum each time. She spoke to nobody unless they spoke to her and then only a few words.

Knell had tried to obtain and sift out a list of those present whilst madame was playing. This had proved an impossible task. In fact, nobody seemed to haunt the gaming-rooms at all. There were a few regulars. Some holiday-makers might come over and over again for a while and then, after a week or two, they were missing because their holidays had ended and they'd gone home.

Madame Garnier, as far as could be ascertained from the casino membership forms and the hotel records, had been the only foreigner playing or staying in the place. Of course, they'd had foreigners there before her arrival and some had arrived since, but nobody at the exact time she was there.

The hotels and boarding-houses had been questioned. There were foreigners appearing on some of their books. Some of them seemed reluctant to admit that their hotels weren't internationally known and they said they'd had visitors from the Continent when they hadn't. After it was all sorted out, there were no French visitors shown in the information gathered for the period Madame Garnier was there, except a croupier at the casino who had an alibi, two young ladies on an *au pair* arrangement and who proved to be fast asleep in Port Erin at the time of the crime, and an acrobat in a sideshow who'd himself been enjoying a night in gaol for getting drunk and disorderly.

The Archdeacon stood beside the one roulette table which was operating, patiently watching the bets and the automatic stereotyped movements of the croupier. He had already read the details of the game from the Gaming Guide and the card handed to him when he entered. He beckoned Littlejohn, who joined him, expecting him to make an excuse for trying a hand at the game himself. Instead:

'Have the croupiers with whom Madame Garnier played been thoroughly questioned?'

'According to Knell's report they were, but had little to tell the police. There were two of them. Is there anything you'd care to ask them?'

'Yes. I think I'd like to meet them and have a talk with them. We might get a little better impression from a flesh and blood interview than from cold print, although Knell seems to have amassed quite a bulky file already.'

The men in question were off duty but handy in the hotel and the Superintendent was able to get hold of them and bring them to the small office where the police had made their temporary headquarters.

Both men had the blasé look caused by their monotonous work. One was tall and etiolated and the other thick-set and swarthy. They were introduced as Leo and Frank, as though they were the familiar friends of everybody.

The sight of a clergyman in gaiters shook them out of their boredom. They both seemed to think the Archdeacon might either be out to convert them from their dubious ways or else to solicit a subscription or some service or other for a good cause. Nevertheless, they must have had pleasant memories of the cloth, for they both smiled and treated the Rev. Caesar most courteously.

No, neither of them had noticed anything peculiar about the old French lady. She had spoken very little and seemed very familiar with casino etiquette and play and never entered into conversation with the croupiers or other players whilst the game was in progress.

Littlejohn was amused by the puzzled way in which Leo and Frank dealt with the Archdeacon. They couldn't understand why a police enquiry should somehow have got in the hands of a clergyman.

'He must be a sort of amateur crank… Like Father Brown,' Leo remarked to Frank when it was all over.

'Who's Father Brown…?' said Frank to Leo.

However, that seemed to be all in the way of general information. Madame had been all on her own, made no friends, indulged in no conversation, played the game, taken her winnings and quietly left the room. The Reverend Caesar started on a fresh track.

'I gather Madame Garnier always had with her a sheet of paper bearing figures and symbols. Did either of you see it?'

'Yes, that's true. But she took good care that nobody saw what was on it. I'd no time to try to see it myself and Leo tells me he was the same. She kept it folded in the palm of her hand and now and then took a long look at it.'

Frank thought it was some system or other she'd worked out. At any rate, he said, it did the trick and she won a nice little packet with it.

Leo shook his head.

'I think it was all a phoney… A blind.'

Everybody looked surprised, except the Archdeacon, who quickly took up the point.

'Why?'

'It was a bit of a mystery to me. I never got a glimpse of anything that was written on the paper, but I did see the paper itself. It was always a small sheet of hotel notepaper with the name of the hotel printed across the top. Twice, I saw her looking blankly at the paper, which she was holding *upside down*. You can't play a system that way. In my opinion, she wasn't following the figures on her bit of paper at all…'

'On the occasion that she looked at the paper wrong way up, did she win considerably?'

'Yes, she did. I particularly noticed it. I've thought about it quite a lot. I can only come to the conclusion that madame was just lucky and held the figures in her hand as a sort of mascot or good-luck charm. Real gamblers are full of all kinds of queer tricks and suspicions. As though lady luck were actually alive and you have to do things to please her.'

The Archdeacon drew up a chair and sat on it. He seemed to be settling down to a thorough investigation.

'Now tell me, Leo or Frank, exactly how did Madame Garnier play?'

'What do you mean?'

'I see from the little book I was so kindly supplied with by the man at the door, that there is a list of odds in roulette; eight categories per single chip, as the technical terminology has it. Which did madame use?'

'Straight up bet on one number.'

'Always?'

'Yes.'

'She never, shall we say, insured her straight up bet by what is described in the Gaming Guide as a split bet or a line or corner bet, or even what is termed here a dozen or column of numbers?'

'No.'

'She must have been sure of herself.'

'She was.'

'Did her luck ever let her down?'

'Yes. Now and then she'd back the wrong number.'

'Did she seem surprised?'

'No.'

Leo had been doing most of the talking, but Frank now interposed.

'I noticed that most times when she lost, she'd hesitated about the number before she placed her bet.'

The Archdeacon looked mighty pleased at that.

'Go on. Frank. What then?'

Frank was surprised.

'Nothing else, sir.'

'Does Leo agree with that?'

Leo nodded.

'Come to think of it, Mr Kinrade, I noticed it, too. Sometimes she looked bewildered; other times she was quite sure about the number.'

'When did she place her money; as soon as you called for bets, or immediately before you called no more bets?'

'She placed her chips at the last possible second. Until then, she looked at her paper hard, as though considering it carefully.'

'Did she seem bright and active as she played?'

Both croupiers looked at each other, wondering what the old man was getting at.

'I see you don't quite follow. Let me put a leading question, then. Did she play frivolously or thoughtfully? Did she, now and then, seem to concentrate deeply?'

Leo understood.

'I see what you mean. It's another way of asking why I think she had the paper in her hand. I'd say if she wasn't using it as a sort of lucky charm, she had it to concentrate on. I mean, she looked blankly at the paper until a number came into her mind. That's my theory. It might sound daft, but there it is.'

'It is not daft at all, Leo. As a matter of fact, you may have come upon a very profound truth.'

Leo looked startled. He was well known to be a very decent chap, but profound truth, as the parson called it, wasn't much in his line. He began to expect an improving talk from the Archdeacon. Instead:

'Leo and Frank have strengthened a theory that was stirring in my own mind. We seem to have struck a very interesting case indeed. Thank you very much, Leo and Frank for your help. The psychology of the gaming tables must be an open book to you…'

The two men left them looking completely baffled.

'What did he mean?'

'Search me.'

The Archdeacon rubbed his hands and put on his hat. They returned to the police station to see Knell.

'I think, Knell, you said you hoped to let me have Madame Garnier's mysterious locked diary tonight. Bring it early and stay to supper. Maggie Keggin has a salmon for us. But neither you nor I have the right to ask whence it came. By the way, Knell, try to borrow a portable roulette wheel and bring it with you. We'll probably need it. We couldn't very well ask the casino to lend us a whole table, could we…?'

4

THE STRANGE MIND OF MADAME
GARNIER

After the rarefied atmosphere of the casino, it was pleasant to return through the countryside to Grenaby. Littlejohn drove the borrowed police car. The sun was shining, a little cool breeze was blowing in from the sea and now and then they had to draw in at the side of the narrow country lane to allow the passage of loads of baled late hay from the upland fields. In the near distance the fields of Moaney Mooar and Ballafada swept up to the purple hills. Difficult to imagine that anyone could wish to murder anybody else on a day like this.

They had left Knell to get on with his routine work in Douglas, but as he said good-bye he handed Littlejohn the locked diary found in Madame Garnier's suitcase. Knell handled it as if it were holy writ.

'The Chief said I might let you and the Archdeacon see it before we send it off for expert examination. I'd like it back as soon as you can manage it.'

Side by side with this treasure was a roulette wheel wrapped in brown paper, for, in the case of requests made by Littlejohn or the Archdeacon, Knell liked to think they were no sooner said than done.

'I found it in the lumber room at the police station. It's a relic from the days when someone tried to run an illegal gaming-house. We raided it. I wish those who were fined and told they'd perhaps better leave the Isle of Man, could see the casino now. They'd have a fit!'

It seemed comic, too, to think of the old parsonage at Grenaby harbouring a roulette wheel and a book of instructions on how to make a quick and easy fortune with the help of it.

The tall trees of the old house cast cool shadows across the lawn and the flower beds were rioting with geraniums. Mrs Littlejohn was reading in a deck-chair with the dog asleep beside her. The dog found it too hot to move, opened one eye, wagged her body in welcome, and then closed the eye again.

'What have you got this time? More clues?' asked Mrs Littlejohn, indicating the brown paper parcel under Littlejohn's arm.

'Shhh… Where's Maggie Keggin?'

'In the kitchen, I think. Have you been poaching salmon?'

'No. It's a roulette wheel.'

'Whatever next! You don't mean to tell me you're going to set up a rival establishment in the vicarage?'

The Archdeacon, who had entered by the front door to unfasten the French window, appeared and beckoned Littlejohn.

'Bring it in this way. I don't feel like arguing with Maggie Keggin in this heat. You needn't look so reproachful, Letty. We've brought this home for the purposes of scientific experiment and nothing else.'

Maggie Keggin's head appeared above them from an open bedroom window.

'What have you got there under your oxter, Inspector, that the Venerable Archdeacon doesn't want to argue with me about?'

'Just a parcel from Douglas, Maggie.'

'So I can see. What's in it that you're so eager to get indoors without me seein' it?'

'A roulette wheel…'

'That will do, that will do, Maggie. Just go inside and close the window after you. I'll come and explain,' interposed the Archdeacon. 'There's a coach party indulging in a mystery tour just crossing the bridge. A most edifying sight to find the Archdeacon of Man being denounced by his housekeeper from an upstairs window… Do as I say.'

The window banged down and the Reverend Caesar hurried inside lest worse should befall him. He was soon back. They unwrapped the infernal machine. Knell had cleaned and oiled it ready.

'Where shall we erect it? If we put it on the dining-table there'll be another uproar. Maggie Keggin regards Knell as responsible for this sinful business and can't wait to get at him when he arrives. We'll move the chess men and put the wheel on the little table.'

Littlejohn had to set the contraption in place with the help of a spirit-level. Then they opened the diary with which Knell had included the key. It was a loose-leaved affair with sheets of stout paper held together by rings. The Archdeacon slipped on his half-moon reading glasses and started to read. Littlejohn sat patiently waiting for the old man to say something, but he remained silent, turning over the pages, grunting to himself, frowning, looking more and more irritable.

Littlejohn quietly left by the French window and joined his wife on the lawn.

'Caesar's dead to the world, reading the old woman's precious diary. Better not disturb him.'

They played croquet for half an hour. Then Littlejohn put his head in at the window. The Archdeacon was fast asleep, his spectacles on the end of his nose and the book, locked again, on his lap.

Knell arrived well before his time. The hullaballoo which greeted him from Maggie Keggin awoke the parson, who seemed to have recovered his good humour. He rescued Knell from his housekeeper and said it was time for tea.

'I see you've got the roulette wheel set up...'

Knell chuckled.

'Maggie Keggin has accused me of corrupting you and says it's wicked to take advantage of your old age to lead you into evil ways.'

'We haven't played at all. In fact, you can take it back with you when you go. We won't need it. Madame Garnier's famous system was spurious — what the croupier called phoney. It was a blind. Cover for something much more interesting and intelligent.'

'Get your tea. It's growin' cold...'

Maggie Keggin placed a large cream cake on the table.

'Perhaps you'll look after the tea now, Mrs Littlejohn. And see that that Knell doesn't eat all my cream cake. He's up to all sorts of evil tricks.'

'I'm taking the roulette back with me when I go, Maggie...'

'If you hadn't, I'd have thrown it out of the front door after ye. And see that there's no playing with it for money. It's my opinion you've started all this to get the Venerable Archdeacon's and the Inspector's money out of them. I knew what it would be once gambling got on the island. The devil let loose...'

The Archdeacon handed Littlejohn the diary and the key.

'There you are, Tom. You won't find the means of making a fortune in it... Open it...'

Littlejohn did as he was told. It was obvious the Archdeacon had taken charge of the case. Knell's face was lost behind a large piece of Maggie Keggin's cream cake. He chewed his way through it and raised his eyes with a startled look.

'Does it give us any hints as to how to solve the murder, Reverend?'

'Not actually, but it explains quite a lot about Madame Garnier's strange behaviour. For example, why she played for only comparatively modest gains. Most people with a profitable system would have swept the board. Not Madame Garnier. She didn't always hit upon the right number. When she did, she gained thirty-five to one. That gave her quite a reserve of winnings; enough to carry her through with a profit until her next number came up.'

'So there was some system, after all, Archdeacon?'

Mrs Littlejohn was as interested as the rest.

'No. Madame Garnier was what would vulgarly be called clairvoyant.'

Littlejohn raised his eyes from the book in his hand. The pages were stout, plain sheets, dated at the top, each bearing four vertical columns of numbers in sequence; column one ran from 1 to 13; column two, 14 to 26; column three, 27 to 39; column four, 40 to 52. The columns were printed. Then, by the side of each figure of the columns was another figure written in ink. The used sides of the cards were arranged face to face in pairs; as the pages were turned, two used cards appeared side by side, then two blank backs, then two more bearing the figures…

'Clairvoyant?'

'Yes, Tom. Compare two of the cards which you find face to face. Take a pair at random.'

Littlejohn flicked the pages.

'Well?'

'You will observe that one card bears written figures in what could be a woman's hand; the other has figures put down by a second person, probably a man. What do you see?'

Littlejohn carefully compared the two before him.

'Some of the figures on the left-hand card tally with those on the right; others don't.'

'How many?'

Littlejohn counted.

'Out of the run of 52 numbers on each card, twenty-eight tally.'

'That's twenty-eight hits. Now look at a pair near the end of the book.'

A pause.

'Thirty-four hits.'

'There, you see. Quite enough to win a nice sum on the wheel.'

Knell's jaw had dropped. He was quite out of his depth. So was Littlejohn, though he didn't show it. His wife was the first to speak.

'But if that means she was guessing the numbers...'

'Not guessing, Letty. *Knowing.*'

'But even then, if Madame Garnier knew the number that came up on the wheel, she wouldn't be able to bet on it, because before the ball comes to rest the croupier calls *rien ne va plus*... No more bets.'

'You say the number that came up. That isn't quite right. She knew the next number *that was coming up.*'

'But that doesn't make sense, sir. It's not reasonable. It couldn't happen...'

Knell brushed it aside. He wondered if the old man had lost his wits. Since his boyhood, Knell had believed the Archdeacon to be a fount of wisdom and reasonableness. Now, at last, time had broken him. He was wandering into his second childhood.

'I don't believe it. It couldn't happen.'

'That, my dear Knell, is what is said of every new wonder. Then, later, it becomes almost commonplace. We are now facing such a phenomenon. Do you see the book in the green jacket in the middle of the shelf? Please bring it. The title's *New World of the Mind*. That's it.'

Knell passed on the book like a hot coal.

'I am not asking you to read this book. You are busy men and haven't the time. I just mention it to say that in the matter of Madame Garnier's games of roulette we aren't entering the never-never land or talking hocus-pocus. This book was written by J. B. Rhine, Professor of Psychology at Duke University, North

Carolina. It removes phenomena like those which seem to be embodied in Madame Garnier's little book from superstition and doubt and puts them on a proper scientific footing. In England, men like S. G. Soal have done and are doing similar work. They are endeavouring to place intuitive impressions, commonly called hunches, in proper perspective and trying to explain them in scientific language. My opinion is that Madame Garnier was what is termed a sympathetic, one who has more than the average number of hunches. She used them to her advantage at the gaming-tables.'

'But what about the diary, Archdeacon? Where does that come in?'

'I think, Tom, it is a record of experiments carried on, let us say, between Madame Garnier and her husband, the late Professor Garnier. As university teachers, they probably came across this new science of parapsychology, tested it out together, and then tried to apply it to the roulette wheel. Fairly successfully, too, judging from madame's winnings.'

'What is the significance of the figures in the book?'

'As far as an actual system of winning at roulette goes, none. But, as you have noticed, as the experiments proceeded, the results became better. They probably proved to madame, and her husband, too, that she could, if she cared to try, successfully use the precognition — the exceptional hunches she got — in gaming.'

'Were the figures in the book obtained from playing roulette?'

'No. If you look at them again, you'll find the results in hand-writing cover only numbers 1 to 13 in each printed column. That indicates a pack of cards; four suits of ten; plus King, Queen and Jack, which were given additional numbers. These experiments in extra-sensory perception, as it's officially called, have been exciting certain psychologists for years. Perhaps Professor and Madame Garnier came upon them and were interested. Packs of cards were originally used. Garnier drew a card at random from the pack; madame guessed what it would be. Then, as they progressed, they found that Madame Garnier had a flair, a hunch, for the game. She had a gift for the type of precognition required. There are many such people, you know. Mediums, for example, when they don't become fakes. The Garniers may have tried it out with a roulette wheel. However, it would appear that until Professor Garnier died, the idea of winning large sums of money didn't enter into the field.'

Knell sat with an empty teacup in his hand, brooding. He might have been thinking of trying it out with his wife and ending as a tycoon. Littlejohn himself was deeply interested. His hunches in certain cases were famous at Scotland Yard! He was wondering vaguely what was at the back of them all. When he caught his wife's smile, he wondered if she knew, by extra-sensory perception, what he was thinking! He shook himself. This was becoming ridiculous!

There was a tough expression on Knell's face. He looked determined to fight the battle for reason and common sense.

'Clairvoyance? You mean to say it was like a spiritualist séance?'

'No, no, no. Nothing to do with being in league with a spirit on the other side. Just the phenomenon of precognition, of knowing what will occur before it actually happens. We all possess it to a more or less extent. Some little, some much. Hunches, instinctive urges, uneasy prognostications… They are now being scientifically investigated, although, as yet, we know very little about whence they come and how.'

'What about the piece of paper with all the figures on it that madame used?'

'You heard the croupier say that she didn't seem to use it. In fact, he'd seen her pretending to follow the figures when the paper was upside down. I think she used it either as a blind to hide the real way she arrived at her number, or else employed it as an object to concentrate upon whilst she waited for the number to enter her thoughts. You recollect, also, that the croupier said that, at times, she looked troubled and then she rarely bet on the right number. That was when the number wouldn't come comfortably and she had to guess or strain. Certainly, if her results were as good at the roulette tables as those shown at cards in the little book, she stood to win quite a considerable sum at each session. She gave up when she grew tired or the numbers didn't come freely into her mind.'

Knell glanced at the roulette wheel on the side table. It didn't need extra-sensory perception to inform them that he was going to suggest a few experiments.

The Archdeacon held up his hand.

'No, Knell. Not that. We've had enough for one sitting. If you start to spin the wheel, you'll be at it all night, to say nothing of causing more ructions from Maggie Keggin, who, without any gift of precognition, I know is about to erupt upon us any moment with…'

He was right. The door opened.

'Have you been playing at the devil's game, because I see your cups are all half full of cold tea? The salmon's ready and *I'm* going to serve it whatever *you* are goin' to do.'

She left the room and slammed the door.

Knell persisted.

'How does all this affect the murder case? I can't see how…'

The Archdeacon's eyes shone.

'It seems to me to indicate enquiries in France. Evian. The universities where Professor Garnier worked, too, perhaps. The doctor has been trying to persuade me to take a holiday. I think I will, if the Superintendent needs any help.'

5

THE VANISHING FRENCHMAN

So far the police had no line to follow and no lead presented
itself.

Whatever system or precognition had been employed by
Madame Garnier, it gave no idea of the motive for the crime.

The old lady knew nobody. This was virtually established by
extensive and patient police enquiries all over the Island.

Madame Garnier had seemed to be a harmless rather eccentric
old woman. She had caused a stir by winning substantially at the
casino. It might have been that knowing this and seeing her
carrying a handbag on the night of the crime had stimulated some
crook or even some hitherto innocent person to relieve her of her
winnings.

But the shooting was a different matter. An armed holdup was
unusual, especially in a place like the Isle of Man, which could be
almost totally sealed off from the outside world in case of emergency. Already police were active at the airport and the packet-
boat piers. To the annoyance or delight of many travellers,
according to their taste in treatment, and the delay in planes and
boats, everyone leaving the Island was subjected to scrutiny and

checking. This screening had come into operation immediately the murder became known.

Everybody likely was interrogated. Nobody saw anybody suspicious about the scene of the crime at the time it was committed. It was all very difficult because the holiday high season had multiplied many times the usual population.

Then, a new development!

As Knell was sitting in his office on the morning following his visit to Grenaby and brooding on the case, his troubled thoughts were disturbed by the weeping — it could have been described as roaring — of a child and the deep barking of a dog. Then the angry voice of their owner.

'Oh, shut-up and stop it! You'll cry yourself into another convulsion if you keep on and then you'll go cross-eyed again.'

And a constable ushered the party into Knell's retreat.

A small, thick-set, worried man. He was dark-skinned and foreign looking. He might have been an Arab or a Cypriot, but he spoke fruity Lancashire. Knell was content to leave that mystery unsolved. He was accompanied by a small boy with butter-coloured hair and livid with yelling, and a large boxer dog. Knell wondered which boarding establishment was putting up with this trio.

The dog gave Knell a sad look, whimpered, and then decided to take a liking to him, leapt across the room and panted all over him. Knell rose to defend himself, as the dog seemed determined to climb up him and lick the top of his head.

Meanwhile the man shook the child until his teeth rattled and in the resulting silent stupor, made himself heard. He rather resembled the dog.

'My name's...'

The attendant constable didn't let him get any further.

'His name's Pennyquick.'

'Walter,' insisted the newcomer.

'Walter Pennyquick. He comes from Accrington and is here on holidays.'

'Got here last Saturday. Came by boat. Never again. Even the dog was sick. We're flying next time, dog an' all.'

It was like an operatic duet. Knell couldn't stand any more of it.

'All right, Casement. He can speak for himself. You can go and get on with what you were doing.'

Casement looked hurt.

'Very well. But before I go, I'll leave this with you, sir.'

And he placed a lady's handbag on the desk with a dramatic gesture.

'Like as not, it belonged to the French woman and is the one we've been searching for. *This* was inside...'

Before Knell could stop him, P.C. Casement opened the bag, gingerly put in a finger and thumb and between them lifted out, like someone removing a bad fish, a small automatic pistol. This he placed on the table with reverent care and then he left the room without another word.

At the sight of the gun, the child emitted a full-throated yell, and started his bellowing all over again. The dog which Knell had persuaded to sit under the desk howled dismally.

The child spoke to his parent in what sounded to Knell like Polish.

His father gave him a hunted look in which Knell read a fleeting desire to murder.

'He says he wants it. It's *his*,' translated Mr Pennyquick.

The child said a few more words in his private gibberish and started to bawl again. Then, in the middle of the row, he suddenly stopped and spoke in decisive plain English.

'I want to go to the toilet.'

Blessed relief! Knell rang the bell for Casement, who eagerly appeared and looked amazed when given his instructions.

'Take him down to the lavatories and show him the cells.'

Anything for a respite. The dog followed the other two underground.

'Now Mr Pennyquick.'

'Dog found the bag under a bush in the Prom gardens...'

Mr Pennyquick looked proud of the fact. It seemed as though he preferred the dog to the child.

'Gun was inside it. Our Rupert's seen guns on the telly and said that one had come from Father Christmas. You see, dog took it, bag and all, to our Rupert and it was quite a while before we found out what he'd got. We'd a job getting him to give it up. Lucky he didn't pull trigger. There'd have been another murder on your books...'

Good-bye to fingerprints if Rupert had given the gun the once-over and his father had tussled with him to recover it.

'I thought we'd better hand it in at police station. So we came right away. His mother's with us, but she's a bit nervous of police. So we left her having an ice cream down the hill.'

'Very proper.'

'I suppose it's gun that shot th'old woman on beach.'

'Probably.'

The child and the dog returned. Casement didn't even show his nose. He opened the door and propelled them into the room from behind. The boy started to yell again at the sight of the gun. The dog eyed the handbag as though about to claim that, too.

Knell gathered the three of them together and manoeuvred them to the door and out. Cocky, the dog, suddenly changed his mind about Knell and bared his teeth at him in farewell.

'Will there be a reward?' asked Mr Pennyquick over his shoulder.

'We'll keep in touch. Where are you staying?'

Walter gave Knell his Douglas address and then, to make sure, his Accrington one, too.

'Just in case you decide to send a cheque after we've gone.

Gun's worth quite a bit, I should think, and after all, we did find it, didn't we?'

Meanwhile, the dog had eaten the sandwiches of a constable who had been called away.

'Be seein' you, then.'

Knell hoped not. He blew out his cheeks and deflated them again.

'What now?'

He tenderly fingered the gun. It was almost vest-pocket size. A snub weapon for work at close range. He opened it and squinted at the magazine. Six cartridges; one fired. The dog and the child, followed by Walter seemed to have disposed of most of the finger-prints it might have held when they came upon it and left their own marks instead. However, best to let the technical boys take a look at it. He rang for Casement again.

'Ask George to see if there are any fingerprints on it. And check that the bullet which killed Madame Garnier came from the empty case in the magazine.'

'You'll be lucky. The kid's been playing with it. Pennyquick must be potty. Lucky the safety catch was on. Did you take the kid's dabs for purposes of elimination?'

Knell had thought about it, but the idea of a pantomime with Rupert in his present state of mind had revolted him.

'No, I didn't. But here's the address of their diggings. You can go round there this afternoon and take them. Take his father's as well. You needn't bother about the dog's paw-prints. And then tell George it's urgent.'

'That damn' dog ate my sandwiches…'

'You'd better buy some more then and take the cost out of the reward money old Pennyquick's demanding.'

Knell, alone again, sat back. He pulled the bag before him. Pennyquick had probably been rummaging in it, but the contents, such as they were, seemed intact. Some odd Swiss and French coins, some loose English change, a silver powder compact and puff with Madame Garnier's initials on it. Spectacles in a spectacle case. A lipstick and a nail file and some orange sticks... Nothing very important. No diary or pencil. No papers or tickets. Knell handled them all very gingerly. Pennyquick and his family had probably mauled the lot very freely and ruined any alien prints which might have been there.

Knell absentmindedly opened the spectacle case. It contained a delicate and expensive pair of lady's glasses in real tortoiseshell. Knell held them against the light and squinted through the lenses. They were obviously reading-glasses, very powerful. He saw the tall old buildings which cut the sunshine from his office through a mist.

A thought struck Knell. He took up the phone and asked for the director of the casino.

'Could you tell me, please, if Madame Garnier wore spectacles when she played roulette?'

'Just a minute, Inspector. I'll have to ask the croupiers...'

The reply came quickly. Madame Garnier didn't wear spectacles.

That was that. And it probably confirmed to a certain extent the theory that madame's scrap of paper containing figures which everybody thought were part of a system, was a mere blind, or else something to help her concentrate and steady her mind whilst she waited for her numerical hunches. She couldn't possibly have read the small figures without spectacles if her eyes were as bad as the spectacles he was holding indicated.

Knell took up the phone again.

'Grenaby Parsonage, please. Superintendent Littlejohn.'

Littlejohn was tidying up the unsightly mess caused by what was going to be the Archdeacon's new solarium. If they were shortly going abroad, he'd better leave everything ship-shape.

Already, the eager Archdeacon had made provisional bookings by plane to Geneva, where they'd stay one night and then go on to Evian by lake steamer.

'Littlejohn here.'

'We've found the gun, sir. It was in the lady's handbag which had apparently been thrown in a bush in the promenade gardens by the murderer in flight. A dog retrieved it and the gun was there inside it.'

'What type?'

'A snub-nosed automatic. The name's Beretta.'

'Loaded?'

'Yes. One cartridge fired. I've sent it down to be tested for fingerprints and a check that the bullet which was fired was the one that killed the old lady. It must have been done at close range. This gun was no good, in my opinion, for distance work.'

'You're quite right, Knell. I know the type. A lady's gun. I wonder if it belonged to Madame Garnier. We'll have to find out. Anything else?'

Knell told Littlejohn about the spectacles and his own views about madame's eyesight. Probably she couldn't read anything small without them and she'd never been seen wearing them at the roulette tables.

'I see what you mean. She couldn't have been reading the pieces of paper with the figures on them. Good for you.'

'Have you anything fresh, sir?'

'The Archdeacon has booked our plane seats for Evian for tomorrow. He's busy packing his bags. And I have been on the telephone to my friend Inspector Dorange, of the Nice Sûreté. I wanted an introduction to his opposite number in the Evian district. It will be Inspector Floret, of Thonon, near Evian. He's an old colleague of Inspector Dorange who has offered to make a trip to Evian and meet us there. Which will be splendid.'

'I remember Inspector Dorange. Wish I were going, too.'

'So do I, but someone's got to remain in charge here... Anything else of interest in the handbag?'

'No, sir. Some coins... Small change. English, French and Swiss.'

'Swiss? You can't gamble heavily in Switzerland. All the same, Evian's in France, but it's very near Swiss territory. Lausanne's not far away. Directly opposite across the lake, and I know a lot of women go shopping there from the French side. We'll bear that in mind. Also, I think I'd better take the murder weapon with me. Will you speed up the examination of it in time for me to have it?'

'Certainly. Somebody over there might recognise it.'

'Anything else in the contents of the bag?'

'Cosmetics. An expensive powder compact, lipstick, handkerchief, nail file... The usual contents of a woman's bag. Nothing of much importance, as far as I can see.'

'Right. Well, we'd better meet again before the Archdeacon and I leave for Evian. Maggie Keggin's conscience seems to be troubling her about the inhospitable way she received you last night. She told me to tell you there's a cold game pie for supper.'

Knell whinnied.

'I'll be there, sir.'

During the conversation, P.C. Casement had entered the room twice, each time bearing slips of pink paper, which he'd placed on Knell's desk. They were reports from various centres of the Island, keeping Headquarters up to date about the search for foreigners and other suspects.

Douglas, Nothing. Ramsey, Nothing. Peel, Nothing. Castletown, No developments.

Knell initialled them one by one and then threw the lot in the waste-paper basket under his desk.

Then he rang for Casement.

'Look, I don't want you wasting your time typing out reports about nothing. Just let me know when something useful comes in, if it ever does.'

Casement bared his teeth to the gums in a joyful grin and with exaggerated care placed before Knell yet another pink slip.

48

Frenchman found unconscious last night at
Cronk-y-Voddy. Report follows. Peel.

Knell flourished the pink paper.

'Is this a joke?'

'No, sir, I just hurried up to tell you. They're taking down the report from Peel police over the telephone downstairs now. The Frenchman was found by the roadside in a state of collapse. He's since vanished.'

6

TROUBLE AT ORRISDAK HALL

At Glen Helen, the north-south road which runs from Castletown to Kirk Michael and Ramsey, rises to a plateau along which is scattered the hill village of Cronk-y-Voddy. Dogs' Hill in English. Various parts of the Isle of Man are haunted by spectral black dogs and this seems to be one of them. On a clear day the view is magnificent. To the right the sweeping backbone of graceful hills and fine valleys; to the left the Mountains of Mourne and the Mull of Galloway across a fabulous blue sea.

Knell had no time for dogs or scenery as he tore along in a police car, on his own, his mind set on reaching *Thie Vraney* and Mrs Craine, who owned it, as soon as possible. He was driving with such speed that he overshot the garden gate before he knew it and had to reverse and crawl back, which took some of the dramatic fizz out of his arrival.

Thie Vraney. TEAS.
Lunches and Dinners to Order.

A double-fronted cottage with a wooden gate, a long path between flower beds, and roses round the door. From the latter there emerged a smell of baking, for Mrs Craine's confections were advertised as Home Made.

Mrs Craine appeared so rapidly at the door that she must have been expecting Knell. She invited him in.

A smallish, stringy, middle-aged, tight-lipped woman who, in spite of the remote peace of her present abode, had had her purple patches in life. In her youth, the beauty of the Cronk, she'd run away to Pittsburgh, Pennsylvania, with a married grocery traveller, done little good there, and, after marrying and burying the grocer, had grown homesick and returned to the Island. She was a shrewd woman and as soon as the Peel police had hinted that her mysterious Frenchman might be connected with the casino murder, had envisaged a rapid increase in her business from curious and hungry tourists eager for any kind of thrill, especially murder. She was, therefore, bubbling over with co-operation.

She propelled Knell into the dining-room, a converted parlour, and offered a chair, one of a uniform lot which had been purchased in an auction-room. Large tables with clean white cloths, each with its cruet and bottle of sauce. The walls were washed in pale blue and decorated with water-colours of Manx scenes, and a notice *The Pictures on the Walls are for Sale.*

Knell introduced himself and stated his business. Mrs Craine did the same by handing him a card.

THE OLD MILLHOUSE CAFÉ (THIE VRANEY)
MRS CRAINE. CRONK-Y-VODDY.
SATISFACTION GUARANTEED.

'Pleased to meet you. I'll just get you a cup of coffee.'

'No. Please don't. I'm in a hurry, Mrs Craine. Sit down, too, and just answer a few questions, will you?'

'The police were here from Peel earlier on. I told them all I know.'

'Yes. I'm in charge of the matter. I want first-hand information, if you don't mind. Now what is this about a Frenchman?'

'It was my granddaughter, Rose, who said he was French. I couldn't tell what he was talking about when I found him. Collapsed at the gate, he was. Rose goes to the High School and when the man started to talk in a foreign tongue, I thought I'd better get her, even if it was nearly three o'clock in the morning. Rose's parents live just over the road. My son and his wife. Rose should be somewhere about. It's school holidays…'

Knell had a feeling that the child was somewhere in the wings ready to make an entrance and play her part.

'Not just now, Mrs Craine. Tell me what happened.'

'It's about the casino murder, isn't it? The constable who made the report to Peel earlier, said it may turn out to be a matter of a murder. And as there isn't any other murder but the one at the casino…'

'About the Frenchman. What was he doing here?'

'On the night of the murder the alarm clock went off by mistake at just before three. I'd been baking during the day and had set it at three in the afternoon, the time the loaves should have been ready. I make my own bread. Everything here is homemade…'

'You woke up at three a.m.?'

'Yes. I wound up the clock when I went to bed and forgot to alter it to wake me at seven in the morning. It's a long day here, you know, in the season and I guess because I was tired, I over-looked it. This is a popular place all the food being homemade and home prepared…'

'Three a.m.'

'Yes. I took a bit trying to sleep and then suddenly I heard the noise at the gate. Somebody groanin'.'

'So you got up to investigate.'

'In the end, I did. Being all alone and the roads occupied by some queer people these days, I thought a bit before I made up my mind. But the groans kept on. So, in the end, I opened the window and called out. "Who's there?" But he only groaned. I have a flashlight in the bedroom and I shone it on the gate. There he was, hanging over it. At first, I thought he was drunk and then I could see that he was ill. He raised himself once or twice and tried to speak and then put his hand over his chest as though there was a pain there.'

'In the end, you went to investigate and found he was ill?'

'Yes. When I opened the gate he fell down in a faint. I didn't care to leave him like that, doubled up on the path. Then, just as I was going to my son's for help, he sort of got half-way on his feet. I helped him up and managed to get him indoors.'

'Then you went for help?'

'Yes. I wakened my son and he came across with me. Rose got up, too, and came with us, because I said the man was talkin' some foreign language and knowing she was learnin' French — she passed her GCE in it — I asked if she'd come and try to make out what he was talkin' about. When we got back, the man was sittin' on the couch, look-in' dazed. He only spoke French once. He asked where he was. Rose said that was French. Then, he sort of came to himself and spoke English with a foreign accent for the rest of the time. He didn't say much.'

'What did he say?'

'He felt better and was all right.'

'Anything else?'

'He asked for a drink of brandy. I don't keep it in the house, but my son had some. He sent Rose over for it. My son said he'd telephone for a doctor. The man got a bit excited and said not to, he didn't need one, he'd soon be all right.'

'What did you do?'

'My son said he wouldn't take the responsibility. And I agreed with him. He might have died on our hands because it was plain to see he'd had a heart attack. Besides, a doctor would have sent for an ambulance and taken him to hospital. I don't know what the man was doing in Cronk-y-Voddy at that time of night, but an ambulance was the only way, to my mind, that he could be got away.'

'So, your son went to telephone...'

'There's a kiosk about a mile off. After my son had left, the man asked me if I'd mind making him a cup of tea until the brandy came. I left him comfortably on the couch. I wasn't away more than five minutes in the kitchen. When I got back, he'd vanished. It wasn't fair of him. Juan, my son, had to go back and telephone the doctor's house. He was on his way, his wife said. He arrived within the half hour and he was very annoyed at being brought out for nothing. As for the man, Juan went out on the road with the torch, but there wasn't a soul about. He'd disappeared, and that was the last of him. When the police from Peel came enquiring earlier today, I told them all about it. The Frenchman might have been concerned with the casino crime. A man who'd do a trick like that on us would do anything.'

'What did he look like?'

'He was tall and fat. Dark, with heavy lips and a big curved nose. He was bald at the front, but had fairly thick hair at the back. Black hair mixed with grey. His face was as white as a sheet when he first came in, but after a bit went pink and more healthy.'

'A long face?'

'No, round and fat. He was a fat man. Very heavy. But he was light on his feet. He got up and made for the door when a doctor was mentioned and my son laid a hand on him and led him back to the sofa.'

'How tall?'

'That's a bit hard to say. If he'd been slim, he'd have been not far off six feet. But bein' so heavy, it sort of reduced his height. You see what I mean?'

'Quite. Anything else?'

'Easy livin', I'd say. He'd beautiful hands, white, and the nails well cared-for. Not what you'd call a working-man.'

'How was he dressed?'

'That was the funny part about it. He'd no hat or overcoat on. I grant you it's summer and it was a nice warm night. But anybody wanderin' about Cronk-y-Voddy without hat and coat at three in the morning is unusual. He wore a dark suit and a white shirt.'

'That's a very helpful description, Mrs Craine. Thanks.'

'I can see him now. We don't as a rule get his sort round these parts. He stands out.'

'The point is, where did he get to? Any ideas?'

'I can only think, and Juan agrees, that he was in a car which was parked a bit down the road. He perhaps felt ill and got out to get help. Then, when he felt better, he went back to the car and drove off.'

'You didn't hear a car?'

'No.'

'Rather a dirty trick, after all the trouble you'd been put to, to sneak off as soon as your back was turned without a word of thanks…'

'I think you and me would forget our manners if we'd murdered somebody and were on the run, wouldn't we?'

'But what was he doing in these parts?'

'I wonder if he was seeking a quiet spot to hide out in till things blew over a bit. There's some wild, lonely country on every side and he might have thought he'd find a suitable hiding-place…'

'That's true. Well, if you haven't anything more to tell me, Mrs Craine, I'll be getting about my business. Thanks very much for your help. I'll not forget it.'

'It's a pleasure. Anyone who'd kill a helpless old woman the way he did deserves all that's coming to him. If there's anything more… Sure you wouldn't like a cup of something before you go?'

'I'm sorry, I haven't the time. When this is all over I'll bring my wife and we'll have a dinner with you.'

'See you do, then.'

Knell's first call on the way back was at the telephone box mentioned by Mrs Craine. There he sent messages gathering a body of police to search the whole countryside around Cronk-y-Voddy and farther afield. Men from the Loyal Manx Association, the Island's squad of special constables, were brought in, too.

As he left the telephone box, Knell found himself confronted by an old colleague, P.C. Tramper, of the Peel force, holding his motor-bike, as though at any time it might leap from his hands like a dog from its leash and bound away from him. A tall cheerful man, his ruddy smiling face framed in a black crash-helmet in which he looked like a visitor from a distant planet. He was an English countryman who had married a Manx girl, who, as so frequently happens, had finally persuaded him to take her to live at home again.

'Morning, Inspector.'

'Morning, Fred. Anything fresh?'

There was something fresh in the forefront of P.C. Tramper's mind. His wife had presented him with a bouncing boy on the night of the murder, but he knew from Knell's predatory manner that his mind was fixed on the crime and some other time would be more appropriate to discuss the newcomer.

'No. I've just been as far as Michael to enquire if any-thing's been heard there about the Frenchman, but I drew a blank. I called at the shops there in case he'd been trying to get food or to telephone, or perhaps some of the gossips might have talked…'

Knell was impatient to be getting back to facts. Tramper's innocent excursions in the neighbourhood weren't in his line just then.

'Tell me, Fred, if you take the Mill House café as the centre of a circle, where would you imagine anybody anxious to disappear, like the Frenchman was, would go? Say, within a short distance, because if he'd had a heart attack, he would not be inclined to walk very far.'

Tramper slowly rotated on his axis, his blue eyes seeking near horizons. 'What a morning and what a view,' he said to himself and then his thoughts returned to duty.

'There are three farms within a short distance. I know the farmers, Bridson, Brew and McTurk. None of them's likely to put up a Frenchman, especially at that time o' night.'

He revolved another forty-five degrees.

'There's cottages all along the main road. If anybody there had been disturbed we'd soon have known it. They all mind one another's business around here and anything unusual, however private it might be, soon becomes common knowledge.'

He turned and faced the West, where the sun was shining across the still, dark-blue sea with the Mull of Galloway lazily extended beyond it.

'Two more cottages and two more farms... Not very likely there.'

Knell was getting impatient.

'We'd better enquire at all of them. I'll phone the Inspector at Peel about it when I get back to Douglas.'

Tramper didn't seem to hear. He was still working on the local topography.

'Then there's Orrisdale Hall. The big square house in the clump of trees there. You can just see the chimneys. It was empty for years and then Colonel Springer, from Kenya, bought it and did it up. He lives there on his own with a housekeeper. I saw him in Michael this morning. He's not the type to harbour strangers. He likes to be quiet and private. He set the dogs on some exploring holiday-makers last summer and landed himself in court.'

Knell pulled the brim of his hat down to indicate that he was going and made for his car. Tramper followed, pushing his bike and still talking.

'The Colonel must be stocking-up for the winter judging from the tinned goods he was buying-in at the grocer's. This is one of the first localities to get snowed-up in winter weather.'

Knell halted in his tracks. He'd recently seen a crime play on television where a man, hiding, had been detected because his old nurse, who was harbouring him, had been causing gossip in the village about her increased appetite.

'Orrisdale Hall, you said?'

'Yes. There's a signpost to Little London down the road there. Across the way there's another road which leads to the highway to Peel. You take that, but half-way along, there's a turn to the right. You go down there for about half a mile and then, on your left is the gate to the track that leads to the hall. It's quite a good road. Want me to come with you?'

Knell didn't want Tramper's company on the visit. He wished to go alone. A policeman in uniform might flush the birds, if any.

'Going back to Peel, Fred?'

'Yes.'

'I'm going the other direction. So I'll wish you all the best and be on my way.'

Fred looked surprised and if his head hadn't been encased in his crash helmet, he'd have scratched it. He wished Knell good luck and made off about his business. Knell paused to light a cigarette and then took the complicated route described by the bobby.

It turned out exactly as Tramper had said. At the end of the last stretch, a sunken road between heather and bracken descended to a sheltered valley. Then a clump of windblown trees, a substantial wall, and a strongly-built squat house beyond.

The place seemed dilapidated, in spite of the Colonel's efforts to make it habitable. A solid gate in the wall gave access to the front entrance of the house. Further along the wall was a postern which Knell, remembering the tale about the dogs, thought he'd perhaps better try first with a view to exploring the lie of the land. The latch was rusty, but the door gave way after an effort.

Knell found himself in the stable-yard, a square cobblestoned derelict place with the old stables and harness room almost tumbling down. In the middle of the yard, an old well-head with a rusty pump on top. There were no dogs about.

Lying on the cobblestones, a spare wheel and a jack and levers for changing a tyre. But there was no car about, either outside or in the stables.

Knell's mind worked quickly. If the Frenchman *had* been staying at Orrisdale Hall, he might have used the car, and, on his way back from Douglas on the night of the crime, had tyre trouble, tried to remove the wheel, then unable to help himself, had had to walk a distance. The strain might have brought on a heart attack. Somewhat recovered, he had sneaked away from Mrs Craine's, reached the hall and had the car brought in. But where was the car now?

It was only a theory, probably exaggerated, but Knell thought he'd better investigate further. There was a door to the house across the yard. Knell crossed and opened it.

'Anybody there?'

Somewhere in the house, he thought he heard the whining of a dog; then silence.

Knell entered gingerly. There seemed to be nobody about. A door across the room stood open. The place must have been the kitchen. Cooking implements, a Calor gas-stove, dirty dishes in the sink. A large empty table and a few chairs in the middle of the room.

Knell called again. No reply.

He crossed and put his head round the other open door.

He remembered nothing else. The roof seemed to crash on his head and he fell flat-out and heavily.

An hour later, the Inspector and a constable from Peel found him, conscious but tied up with a piece of dirty rope and a handkerchief between his teeth. Tramper had reported his meeting with Knell and anticipating his orders from Douglas, had set out at once on a tour of enquiry. Knell, still slightly concussed and rambling a bit, told them what had happened and they rushed him to hospital in Douglas for examination. He was put to bed to recover, in spite of his protests that he was all right and had urgent duties to perform. When his chief promised to tell Littlejohn what had occurred, he ceased complaining and fell asleep.

In a nearby bed, a hardened criminal and frequent adversary of Knell lay dying from heart trouble. As the mists gathered round him, he heard voices which seemed to him to be those of angels, until they announced the arrival of Knell in an unconscious condition. The shock provided a stimulus to the thief's flagging heart. He began to improve right away and before Knell was fully recovered, he had resumed his wicked ways.

7

COMMOTION AT SEA

I t was only after they had comfortably disposed of Knell that the two policemen from Peel began to investigate the house itself. They were in for another surprise.

They found Colonel Springer trussed-up under the stairs and gagged so efficiently that he hadn't been able to make even the slightest noise to warn Knell or the men from Peel of his enforced presence there. Someone had made a professional job of him. His eyes bulged like organ stops, his face seemed split into two parts by the tightness of the gag, and his arms were bound to his legs like a chicken ready for the spit.

'The bloody swine!' said Springer as they removed the gag. They cut his bonds and he collapsed in a heap, unconscious.

The policemen seemed overwhelmed in a mass of work. Springer unconscious; Knell on his way to hospital half-dead; the Frenchman who, they assumed, had been the cause of the commotion, probably in full flight; and the case of the casino murder overhanging it all.

Tramper hooked off his helmet and mopped his head all over. Traa di Liooar! Time enough! The Manx tempo which usually absorbed everyone who came to the Isle of Man, natives, visitors and retired residents alike. It didn't, as yet, seem to have caught up the Frenchman!

They dealt with Springer first. Tramper found some brandy among a staggering amount of alcohol — mainly whisky — in the sideboard cupboard. On his way back to the scene of activities, he took a little nip himself. He felt he'd earned it. They shook the unconscious man into a semblance of life and then, after making sure that he could swallow, they gave him a swig of the brandy. He coughed, sat up, and asked for more. So, they gave him another dose.

Springer made motions to the Inspector to come nearer as he wished to make some statement or other.

'Where are the dogs?' he whispered hoarsely.

'I don't know, sir. They sounded to be disappearing in the distance, judging from their barking when we arrived.'

Springer reared himself up angrily.

'Oh, hell!'

'Have they been stolen?'

'No. They're bitches and it's mating season with 'em. Now they'll go and produce a lot of blasted little mongrels fathered on 'em by all the curs in the locality. What happened?'

He didn't seem to know! He must have been badly concussed. They gave him more brandy. Then he put his hand on the top of his head and shouted with pain and rage.

'Here! That swine Allasac must have knocked me out. I'll kill him for this. There's a lump on my head like an egg. Where is he?'

'Perhaps you feel well enough now to tell us what's been happening, sir.'

The Inspector helped Springer to his feet from the floor where he'd been squatting, pending complete recovery, like a fakir emerging from a trance.

He was a medium built man, thick set, with a round face now drained of blood and netted with purple veins. He was bald at the front and had a fringe of sandy hair behind his head. A dark bristling moustache, thick eyebrows and bulging blue eyes now filmed by the copious doses of brandy he'd absorbed.

Springer groped for a chair and sat heavily on it. He asked for more drink.

'Whisky this time. Any more brandy and I'll be sick all over the place. My head feels the size of two and I've got cramp in all my limbs. Why didn't you fellahs come before? Never there when you're wanted.'

Tramper solemnly pouring whisky in a glass and casting about for some soda, flushed with emotion. As a rule, the police weren't particularly popular, yet here was a chap who seemed to want them in permanent residence, just in case...

'Neat, man. Neat. I can't stand soda. Neat.'

The Inspector was annoyed, too.

'Do you mind telling us, Colonel Springer, exactly what's been going on? If, as you say, you've been attacked and tied-up, whoever did it is getting away. We're wasting time.'

It seemed to trigger-off a convulsion of recollection in Springer. He started to supply a spate of information, his arms waving, his body heaving, and now and then, he broke into a string of horrible obscenities. He thrust his face close to those of his listeners as he talked, and blew blasts of alcohol over them.

Shorn of indecencies of speech, it boiled down to this:

During the war, Springer had been parachuted into France...

Sitting there, dishevelled and covered in the dust of the glory hole under the stairs, he looked as if he'd been parachuted down his own chimney!

...Springer had been parachuted into France to contact the underground at Grenoble. There, in the wilds of the Grande Chartreuse, he'd encountered a number of university teachers, all of them under assumed names. One of these had been Allasac, a brilliant surgeon, who had attended to the wounded. Interrupted and pressed for a description of the man, he gave a good one, embellished by every term of abuse to which he could lay his tongue.

'It's the Frenchman!' shouted Tramper, as though he'd solved the whole problem.

'Of course he's a Frenchman! What the hell do you think he'd be in the circumstances?'

Allasac had unexpectedly turned up at Orrisdale Hall two days before. He said he'd been on a visit to England and had called at the Isle of Man to see his old comrade of the *Maquis*.

'Just like that! As though the Isle of Man were a mere bus ride out of London and he and I were like David and Jonathan. I never liked the fellah. Bit of a dark horse and I never trusted him.'

Springer took another gulp of his whisky with one hand and pawed the air with the other to indicate he didn't wish to be interrupted.

'He asked if I could put him up for a night as he couldn't get a plane booking to London until the day after. I was amazed at his damned cheek. Why couldn't he have stayed at a hotel? But what could I say? I couldn't just chuck the fellah out. I've no help here at present. Housekeeper's had to go to Andreas to nurse a sister who's dying. I told him he'd have to pig it. He seemed delighted. Said we'd pigged it before in the Grande Chartreuse in the old days. Why not again?'

'What was his real name?'

'Damned if I know. Didn't ask him. Called him Allasac. just as we used to. Funny thing. It was the rule that we only addressed one another by our *nom de guerre* in the old days of the Resistance. Precaution, you know. Never knew who was who, you see. We fell into the habit right away. He called me Grimaud, which was my working name when I was with 'em...'

'But he must have known your real one. How else could he have enquired where you lived? Unless, of course, you'd kept in touch.'

'That's true. We didn't keep in touch. I was glad to see the last of him when it was all over. Queer customer. He must have got my address from the telephone book after he got here. I like his nerve!'

'How did he know you were in the Isle of Man?'

'I do keep in contact with a number of my old French friends of those times. Matter of fact, there's a sort of club. He could have got my address there.'

It seemed that Allasac's cheek had no limit. He'd borrowed Springer's car to go to Douglas, whence, he said, he wished to cable home to say that he had been delayed.

'Delayed! You're tellin' me! He said he had an international driving-licence, so I agreed very reluctantly. The swine didn't get back here till nearly four o'clock in the morning. I thought he'd either wrecked the car and killed himself, or else hocked it and beetled off with the money. And he was in a shocking state when he did get here... Fill up my glass, will you?'

Tramper marvelled at Springer's capacity for alcohol. He just mopped it up and didn't seem a bit different.

'Where was I? The state he was in when he returned. He said he'd had a tyre blow-out at Glen Helen, tried to walk home, and had a sort of heart attack through hurrying up Creg Willey's Hill. I wasn't a bit surprised. He's such a mountain of flesh. Bet he turns the scale at eighteen stones. He'd left the car at Glen Helen, he said, as he didn't know how to change the wheel. I was boiling mad at him. I didn't want the car leavin' there, unlocked, all night. So, I went back on my bike to bring it in. I was all in when I got there...'

Tramper looked thoughtfully at the almost empty whisky bottle. Probably tight when he got to Glen Helen after waiting for the Frenchman till four a.m.

'I felt so done-up and sick of the whole business that I drove the car slowly home on the flat tyre. Changed it this morning. Had to do. I'd very little in the way of food in stock and had to make a trip to Michael to get Allasac's breakfast. I thought I'd better see him off hospitably. What did I get in return? A biff on the head, tied up, gagged, and left to rot. I might have died.'

'By the way, sir, the car's not in the yard. There's a spare wheel and some tools there, that's all. Your friend must have taken it off again.'

The shock of it gave Colonel Springer the final fillip he needed for recovery. He sprang up and reeled away into the courtyard. There he was seized with a violent frenzy. He ran from one shed to another, in and out of the old harness room and back again into the fresh air.

'He's taken the car… Here! Is that your car at the gate? Take me to Peel right away. The fuel cans for my boat have gone, too. I think he's pinched my cabin cruiser, as well.'

'Did he know you had one?'

'Yes. I was daft enough to tell him about it last night and he seemed very interested and asked a lot of questions. Well, what are we waiting for? Are you interested in the theft of a car and a boat or are you not?'

They made for Peel by all the short cuts they knew and arrived there in less than fifteen minutes. The sun was shining, the beach was crowded with families enjoying it all, and the ruined castle and cathedral added a touch of benevolence and security to the background. The peace was shattered by the arrival of a police car driven at high speed along the promenade. The holidaymakers suddenly became animated, rushing here and there, trying to find out what it was all about.

A group of fishermen gathered round the barometer at Munn's Corner near the harbour slowly disintegrated and gaped at the car as it pulled-up.

'It's Colonel Springer and the poliss. Have they been arrestin' him?'

Springer leaned out of the window. He looked ready to have a stroke from the alcohol and the tension of events.

'Hi, you! Hi, Kelly! Has anything happened to my boat?'

'Somebody must have taken her off before I came here this mornin'. She wasn't at her moorin's, but your car was parked nearby, so I reckoned you'd gone off for some fish for your dinner.'

The Inspector slipped in the clutch without more ado. Springer bumped down in the back seat.

'What the hell are you doing? Aren't we going off in pursuit?'

'Where do you expect to catch him? Yours is a fast boat, isn't it? We're going to the police station to telephone details to headquarters at Douglas. They'll do the interception. I've a good idea where your friend might be making for.'

'Where, if it isn't too much to ask?'

'Dublin.'

'The airport!'

'That's it. It's the only way he can get off the Island now. All traffic out of here is watched on account of the murder.'

'What about my car? It's been left in the park at the quay.'

'It's safe there, isn't it? Now that your friend's levanted, there's nobody else likely to pinch it.'

They reached the police station and sent the news to Douglas.

Knell was back in his office, looking somewhat the worse for wear and a bit bewildered. The doctors at the hospital had forbidden him to leave and ordered him to remain in bed, but he'd refused. Finally deciding that his condition might only worsen if they upset him anymore, they'd granted him conditional release. Already he'd broken all the conditions.

Littlejohn and the Archdeacon were with him and, in a muddled way, Knell was trying to put his adventure of the morning in proper order. The news from Peel seemed to shed light on his problems.

'That explains it all. The Frenchman killed Madame Garnier, made for his friend's house where he intended to hide out until the heat was off, and then, learning that the colonel had a boat, he made up his mind either to run for Dublin in it or else he might be planning to make his way home to France…'

Already news had gone out by radio, and traffic between the Island and Ireland was being watched. Ships in the vicinity were looking out for Springer's cabin cruiser and ports round the English and Irish coasts had been alerted. Knell was almost biting his nails with anxiety.

'I hope he doesn't give us the slip after all. He seems to be a man of action in spite of his weight…'

He instinctively patted the lump at the back of his head very gently.

Littlejohn was anxious about Knell.

'Look here, old chap. If you won't stay in hospital, I'm going to drive you home. If you continue like this, you're going to make yourself very ill. The case is in the very competent hands of your chief, now. And, if it will put your mind at rest, the Archdeacon and I will postpone our trip to Evian until you're fit to be about again. A few days' rest and you'll be all right. We'll keep you informed of progress. The case doesn't seem far from solution now. If we can lay the Frenchman who calls himself Allasac by the heels, we've probably got our man. Come along…'

Knell seemed too all-in to resist any further. He rose unsteadily and put on his hat.

'Right.'

Casement interrupted them. He had another of his pink slips in his hand. He looked surprised to see Knell leaving already.

'There's a message just arrived I think you'd like to see before you go, Inspector.'

Knell gave him a wan look.

'Tell me what's in it, Casement.'

'The *Manx Maid* bound for Dublin on a day excursion has radioed in. Ten miles south-west of Peel, she spotted a vessel on fire. She changed course, but before she was half-way there, the boat blew up. They manned one of the boats and sent her to investigate. There was nothing but wreckage left. No sign of a body. After searching carefully around, they found nothing. Assumed that the man aboard dived in the water. He must have been drowned. The usual air and sea searches will be continued. The *Manx Maid* continued on her course. Quite an adventure for the trippers aboard.'

Knell staggered a bit.

'So, it looks as if he didn't give us the slip after all. I suppose now, Superintendent, your trip abroad will be off.'

'I think not, Knell. As soon as you're well enough to hold the fort again, we'll be going, just to complete the picture.'

8

A MAN ON HIS OWN

After seeing Knell safely home and in bed, Littlejohn and the Archdeacon set out for Cronk-y-Voddy. They were accompanied by James Perrick, a young artist who now and then drew caricatures of Island personalities for the local newspapers. He was particularly interested in police work, the sketching of portraits from mere descriptions without at all seeing the subject. They called at Mrs Craine's café again.

It was a fine evening, a sunny end to a good day, and the place was well filled with diners.

'We won't keep you very long, Mrs Craine. But this is a matter of extreme urgency and I hope it won't disturb your business to talk with us.'

'That's all right, sir. My daughter-in-law and Rose are here and will see to the service. I have a cook in the kitchen and if I'm not away long, there'll not be much delay.'

The patrons of the place didn't mind if it took all night. Someone had recognised the Archdeacon and, by inference, his companion. To be able to tell their friends that, in dining at the Old Millhouse last night, they'd seen the Scotland Yard detective and the Venerable Archdeacon in full cry on the casino murder hunt, was a thrilling sauce to the meal.

'We'd perhaps better have Rose with us. She saw the man who's now known as the Frenchman here, didn't she?'

'Yes. And a bright and observing girl she is too. She should be a big help.'

Rose arrived. Her age was given as fifteen, but she looked nearer twenty. A bright and sophisticated schoolgirl, with her hair done by a professional and even lipstick of the wrong tint on her lips.

As the ground floor was fully occupied, Mrs Craine suggested they should adjourn to one of the bedrooms upstairs and after a preliminary disappearance, presumably to make the place ship-shape, she invited them to follow her.

The interview was long and detailed. Perrick took control and slowly and patiently drew from the two women a description of Allasac, which he first put down in writing.

There was some argument between Mrs Craine and her granddaughter about several details. Perrick tactfully eliminated the objections between the two of them. Rose invariably won the argument. She was taking art at school and seemed gifted with a fairly good photographic memory.

The final picture as built-up by Perrick covered a man of between fifty-five and sixty years of age. Six feet in height. Very heavily built. 'The fattest man I've ever seen,' said Rose. Yet nimble on his feet for all that. Bald in front and with hair slowly thickening as it reached the crown of the head and then a bit bushy and unkempt behind and over the ears. Dark, probably brown eyes, large ears fairly well set back on his head. Shape of head, round, rather like an orange. Nose, Roman. Features, heavy, chin square, lips wide and full, with a slight folding downwards of the nether lip. Yes, a pouting expression, that was it. Colour of hair? It was grey. Must have been dark, almost black once. Complexion? Difficult to describe, as he was obviously ill when the pair of them had seen him. Pale, then, with smooth cheeks the skin of which began to sag around the sides of the mouth and chin and ended up in a small dewlap under the chin.

Excellent! Now for the other features.

The man had nice hands, which he couldn't keep still through gesticulating. The hands were long and slim, in contrast to the man's figure. One hand seemed to have been damaged. There was blood on the knuckles, as though he'd been trying to repair something and barked them. This, Littlejohn, commented, must have been when he found the tyre of the car was burst and tried to do something about it. He was formally dressed in a dark suit with white linen — or rather it had been white. He looked to have been under the car, or something, or else had collapsed in the road from his heart attack and he was dusty and dishevelled.

Most of the time Allasac was in Mrs Craine's house, he had seemed physically distressed and ill at ease, but he had been impeccably polite and had appreciated anything done for him, in spite of the fact that he'd sneaked off without a word of thanks when he'd got the chance.

'He was good class and very clever-looking, in spite of his condition,' said Mrs Craine.

'I think that should be all, for the present,' said Perrick. 'I won't detain you from your business, but if you don't mind I'll make a start with my drawing here and then you can see it and both comment on it when I've made the first attempt.'

Mrs Craine told him and his companions to make themselves at home and she and Rose quietly left them as though something awesome were about to begin. Downstairs again, Mrs Craine maintained a portentous silence when questioned by her clients. 'It's confidential,' she said, but added, 'perhaps next time you come, I'll be able to tell you all about it.'

Which did her future business a lot of good.

Perrick worked quickly and carefully and shortly produced his first draft of the Allasac portrait. This was ruled a bit at variance with 'himself', as Mrs Craine called Allasac, but Rose, with her better training in art, was able to suggest a few corrections. A second draft, a third, and yet a fourth were submitted before both women were satisfied.

Littlejohn thanked Mrs Craine and Rose as they left.

'I'm very grateful for your trouble. By the way, one more question. Did your visitor *say* he'd had a heart attack?'

'Yes. Distinc'ly. He even said he'd a bit of a weak heart and been overdoin' it. Said he walked a long way after his car broke down.'

'Did he look as if he'd had such an attack?'

'In what way?'

'Was his breathing difficult, his lips blue, did he seem faint? I'm sure you've met people with heart trouble, Mrs Craine.'

'Come to think of it, he seemed more as if he'd had a fall. I thought he'd had this attack and fallen down with it. Then managed to drag himself here for help. After all, from Creg Willy's Hill to here is a long stretch; two miles about. A heavy man like that with a bad heart.'

'Did he seem stiff and sore as he dragged himself about?'

'Yes. So would you be if you were as big and heavy as he was and you weren't so well from heart trouble at the same time.'

'Thank you very much.'

Littlejohn turned right on the way back and drove along the single tumbledown track to Orrisdale Hall, visible in the distance through its ring of weary-looking trees. As he opened the gate of the yard, the dogs in the house began to bark aggressively.

'Why they've suddenly started calling it a hall, I can't think,' remarked the Archdeacon. 'Status symbol, I guess. It's really a large farmhouse which has long since shed off its land to neighbouring farmers. Then, it became a manor. Now, it's been promoted again, to a hall. And why Orrisdale? Orrisdale's miles away. In my young days this place was called *Thalloo Losh t...* the burnt land... Whether a fire-raiser lived here or not, I never found out... Here we are. The Colonel seems to be cleaning his car.'

He was. Flinging buckets of water over it because the pump was out of commission and the hall only boasted a spring and there wasn't enough force to run a hosepipe. The Colonel seemed quite good tempered about it.

'Hullo. A fresh squad of police, judging from the look of you, although I wouldn't have thought you'd have needed the chaplain on a job like this. I thought your case finished with the death of Allasac. It's obvious he did the murder. What do you want of me now? Want me as a witness or to give you a statement?'

'That's it, sir. May we come in?'

'Sure. This way.'

He took them through the kitchen now in the records as the scene of Knell's violent adventure.

Springer led them into the living-room. There were piles of dirty dishes, which gave the impression that the housekeeper was still sick-nursing.

Outside, the weather was changing. A wind from the West tortured the trees and was blowing in a mist which began to cover the tops of the hills. The distant sea was just visible now, the colour of old lead.

Springer still seemed surprised to see them. He was clad in old khaki shorts and a sweat-stained shirt. He needed a shave.

'Sorry I'm in such a mess. My housekeeper's returning tomorrow. Been away nursing a sick sister in Andreas who's now been removed to the cottage hospital. Sit down, please. Drink?'

He'd been drinking quite a lot himself but when they refused, he helped himself to some more whisky.

'Dry work cleaning a car with only primitive services. The dam' thing was plastered with mud after Allasac's escapades in it.'

He looked from one to another of them.

'Sorry I was a bit rude, Reverend, when you arrived. I'd no idea you were the bishop...'

'I'm not. Merely Archdeacon. But don't let that worry you. My friend Superintendent Littlejohn is good enough to take me around with him now and then to give me a change of air...'

Springer looked keenly at Littlejohn.

'*The* Littlejohn?'

'Yes.'

'Scotland Yard, eh? What are you doing on the case? It's not as important as that, is it? Surely the island police can handle a matter like this.'

'Of course they can. I am here on a holiday. They're friends of mine and I'm helping with the routine.'

'I see. What can I do for you, then?'

Littlejohn filled and lit his pipe.

'I called to look around, with your permission, Colonel. Just to see if your French friend has left any traces behind him and also to ask you to take a look at a portrait which Mr Perrick here has built up from information supplied.'

'The Peel chaps gave the place a pretty thorough onceover, but I guess you want to confirm it. I'm very willing to do all I can. My main interest in the case now, however, is what are the insurance company going to do about the theft and loss of my boat? Is this the picture?'

Perrick passed it to him.

Springer carefully scrutinised it and then laughed. It was a forced, nervous noise.

'Excuse my mirth. I was just thinking I wish Allasac could have seen this. He'd have had another heart attack. In spite of his weight, he rather fancied himself. A bit finicky and particular about his appearance and looks. All the same, I must confess that if Mr Perrick never met him, it's damned good. But you've given him the appearance, the stark look of a typical criminal having his picture taken before they chuck him in the cells.'

'It isn't a studio portrait. It's simply a composite effort built up...'

'Don't get me wrong. For its purpose, it's just the thing. It only amused me because Allasac was such a dandy in his way and here he looks as if he'd been... well... rolled in the road. His hair's rough, his eyes are more bulging than in actual fact, and his collar and tie aren't as natty as he usually wore 'em.'

'You must remember the people who described him saw him after he'd collapsed from a heart attack.'

'Who did see him?'

'Mrs Craine and her granddaughter. She keeps a café on Cronk-y-Voddy. Allasac fetched up there after he'd walked from your car near Glen Helen and had a heart attack on the road.'

'Have you any suggestions to make which might improve this picture of your friend, sir?'

'Don't be funny, Superintendent. He was no friend of mine. You know what brought him here. Hiding from the police after he'd committed a murder. And you know what he did to me. Slugged me, pinched my car and boat and then set the boat on fire. Now he's dead, so there doesn't seem much point in flogging a dead horse, does there?'

'We don't know he *is* dead. He just disappeared with your boat and vanished from the scene after it got on fire. He might have been picked up by a passing vessel. There were plenty in the vicinity. He might have deliberately fired the boat to put us off his tracks. He must have been making for Dublin, judging from the route he took.'

Springer remained silent.

'Well, if you care to take a look over the place, I'll be very glad to show you. You'll find nothing. He didn't pinch the silver or the cashbox. Just my boat and some cans of fuel. Oh, and a suitcase full of food. Must have been planning, or pretending to plan quite a trip. Come on, I'll show you over.'

It was a solidly built place, with three good rooms and kitchen quarters downstairs and a wide staircase leading from a spacious hall to a landing with four doors. The two dogs, about which the

Peel Inspector had reported in his account of his visit, were sitting in the hall, very subdued, after their recent adventures.

'I see the dogs are back,' said Littlejohn.

Springer gave Littlejohn a sharp look.

'You police don't miss much, do you?'

The animals, two fine smooth-coated, brown Labradors, hesitated and then sidled across to their master, who ignored them. It was obvious that relations were a bit strained.

There seemed to be no sense in searching the place for traces of Allasac. Littlejohn had merely wanted to get a correct idea of the house in his mind. No use trying to imagine a place in which you have to live mentally in connection with a case.

Many of the rooms were unfurnished. There was a small, snug room off the kitchen downstairs, presumably occupied by the housekeeper, and Springer's living quarters, sparsely but comfortably filled in bachelor fashion. Armchairs, a settee, bookshelves, dining-table and sideboard. There were two good-looking sporting guns in one corner and some fishing tackle.

Upstairs, there was one bedroom simply, almost austerely furnished, apparently for the colonel, and another more comfortable and fussy, probably the housekeeper's. A third room with an iron bedstead, a bare mattress and very little else.

'Which room did Allasac occupy during the brief time he was here?'

'Mine, Superintendent, and it was damned inconvenient. I had to turn in the housekeeper's room. She was away. I didn't like it, but I wasn't going to sleep in the spare room or on the couch down below...'

The views from the upstairs rooms were magnificent. The sea, in various aspects, was visible from all of them approached by long stretches of moorland and cultivated fields. On a clear day, there must have been views of Peel, and Ireland or Scotland, according to which of them you occupied.

Springer opened all the doors and showed them the rooms. It

was like conducting would-be tenants or buyers on a tour of inspection. Except that Springer didn't like it.

When they returned below, the Archdeacon sat in one of the armchairs of the living-room and crossed his gaitered legs. He looked settled for a long stay.

'Have a drink, Archdeacon? Make yourself at home.' Springer said it in a slightly sarcastic tone. He was surprised when the Reverend Caesar accepted his offer.

'A little whisky, please, and a lot of soda…'

It ended in whisky for all four of them.

'What made you settle here, Colonel? A bit large and remote for a solitary man like yourself, isn't it?'

'Well you see, Archdeacon, I got it cheap… and it's quiet. There's plenty of good rough shooting, some grouse and rabbit, fishing in the vicinity. Easy access to Peel, not very far from Douglas. I can be left in peace to read my books in the evenings and not be disturbed by visitors intruding. Also, I can write up my memoirs when I'm in the mood.'

'You're writing a book?'

'You might call it that. I've lead a pretty interesting life. Some people might like to hear about it if I can find a publisher to take it on.'

'Very interesting. I wish you luck. Will it principally deal with your adventures with the French Resistance during the war? I heard you were involved in that.'

Springer nodded gravely and took a good drink of his whisky.

'Yes. I'm putting that in. But, of course, there was plenty of adventure before that. I began life in a bank. That should give my memoirs a good start. Light relief, you know. I soon got out of banking. Joined the army to see the world. Trained as a commando and then when war broke out, was moved to intelligence. That's how I came to be mixed up with the resistance movement… But I'm telling you all the contents of my book. You must buy one if it ever comes out.'

Littlejohn intervened.

'You say you met Allasac in the French underground movement. What was the nature of his work there?'

'He was a brilliant surgeon and looked after the sick and wounded of several groups in the district, working under the Grenoble headquarters. I was with the Grenoble squad up in the Grande Chartreuse and Allasac often came there in the course of his duties. We got to know one another pretty well. After all, we were isolated together up there. You get to know your companions.'

'What was his real name?'

'I never knew it. Probing for personal information just wasn't done. If a man fell in the hands of the Gestapo and cracked under their usual interrogation, he might easily betray not only his comrades, but their relatives in the locality if he knew who they were. It was a wise precaution.'

'So you didn't know much about his civil life or where he lived?'

'No. He was a cultured man. He might have been a university teacher or professor of surgery. Grenoble has a large and famous university and quite a lot of the staff were in the Resistance.'

'Did you like Allasac?'

'Can't say that I took to him. He was always on his dignity, a bit standoffish and superior when he came to the Chartreuse to see us. Very conscious of his position as consultant surgeon. Also, he didn't like me much, as though he thought I'd betray the whole set-up any minute. There were some of them like that. They resented outside intrusion. That's why I was surprised when he turned-up here, all amiable and smiling. We might have been bosom pals all our lives. It was simply because he wanted to hide out here. He judged it wise to be pleasant, I guess.'

He slapped the cork in the whisky bottle and put it away in the sideboard.

'Will there be anything more? I must finish the car before it starts to rain. Not looking so good outside. Mist and cloud growing thicker.'

The three visitors rose and Springer shook hands with them all.

'Glad to be of any help, although your visit mustn't have been very productive in the way of information on your case. However, hope to see you again one day.'

He turned to Littlejohn.

'Shooting man?'

'Yes, when I've the time. The only time nowadays is when I come over here.'

'Come up one day and we'll see what we can find. Got your gun here?'

'Not this time.'

'I'll lend you one. Give me a ring when you're free. I'm on the phone.'

He led them to the yard and saw them off with a cheerful wave of the hand.

Once free of the hall, Littlejohn turned to Perrick.

'You've been very quiet, Perrick. Been taking it all in?'

'Yes. Very interesting. Quite a character, the colonel.'

'Care to make a portrait of him, like the one you did of his pal, Allasac?'

'I don't mind if I do. A fine type for caricature. But, then I guess you don't want a caricature.'

'I do not...'

Perrick was so eager to try his hand, that he got busy in the car with pad and pen and before they reached Douglas, he showed Littlejohn a first-rate portrait, warts and whisky and all.

9

THE GARNIER FAMILY

L ittlejohn and the Archdeacon were two days behind in their
trip to Evian.

Knell was still suffering from mild concussion after his blow
on the head on the morning of their intended departure.
Forbidden by his chief to return to duty, Knell developed a stubborn intention of going to Grenaby to begin work on the
Archdeacon's new conservatory. This idea had somehow got
mixed up with the case in Knell's mind and it seemed to him that
one would not be completed without the other. It was not until
evening that he ceased from pestering his wife to bring back the
trousers which she had confiscated and carefully hidden. Then, he
fell asleep and when he awoke the following morning he was
himself again, albeit still unfit for duty, and he could not
remember his struggles of the previous day on behalf of what he
persisted in calling the greenhouse. As he was now reasonable and
promised to rest in bed until their return, Littlejohn and his
friend left the Island by the mid-morning plane to Geneva.

Dorange, Littlejohn's friend of the French Sûreté at Nice, was
waiting for them, with a police car and a tall stranger in uniform
whom he introduced as Inspector Floret, of the Sûreté at

Thonon-les-Bains. Dorange was wearing his famous off-white suit and snakeskin shoes and belt, so well-known to their discomfiture by all the malefactors of the Côte d'Azur. The usual red carnation was in his buttonhole, the symbol of his love for his native Nice.

Dorange and Floret made a strange-looking pair. The man from the South small, swarthy, sparkling with energy; Floret lanky, grey-haired, gangling and sombre as though completely disillusioned and expecting more to follow. He was an old friend of Dorange from their days in Paris and as they were both chain-smokers, they spent half their time offering cigarettes to one another.

Dorange enthusiastically embraced Littlejohn, hesitated, and then embraced the Archdeacon as well. They had met before and had a great admiration for each other. Then Dorange introduced his colleague, who suddenly brightened up and smiled for a change.

'I have a long list of neglected holidays due to me, Tom. I'm drawing on it to spend a few days with you and help if I can. The seaside is no change for me, so Evian is very attractive to me. We may manage some leisure together between working hours. Evian is a great place for horse riding… Or would you prefer its baths and régime of mineral waters…?'

The Archdeacon smiled. He could imagine what the four of them would look like as a posse of horsemen.

'Strange as it may sound, Dorange, I am the only one of us dressed in riding attire. My gaiters are a survival of the days when Archdeacons rode on horseback to various parts of their domain…'

Floret, who was a Catholic, eyed the old man in astonishment. He had never been to England, let alone the Isle of Man, of the situation of which, geographically, he hadn't the least notion. In his mind he saw the clergy of the British Isles pelting along on horseback in search of sinners, just as his own priests did on bicycles, ladies' models, to prevent their soutanes getting mixed up in the works.

They gathered in the large police car which took the road on the French side of the lake, a pleasant run along the foothills, with the giants of the Savoy Mountains on the right, and occasional glimpses of the lake on the left. At Thonon, they halted at a hotel with a great reputation for good food and for training apprentice hoteliers and with a terrace facing the lake. Floret had ordered a special meal for them. They ate braised trout au champagne, poulet aux herbes de Savoie, and crêpes soufflés au Grand-Marnier, and drank Digny, a rare wine, available only to a select few, including the police.

Such a repast precluded all discussion of crime and they spent the time in small talk and the enjoyment of the company, food and wine.

Littlejohn reminded Dorange of a similar gourmets' feast which they had enjoyed at *Le Coq qui Chante* in Cannes, in company with Inspector Audibert, of Marseilles and Cromwell, of the Yard.

'Some friends of mine, who were leaving for a holiday on the Coast, asked for the menu in every detail. They ordered at a famous restaurant on the way to Nice. The bill came to almost twenty-five pounds for two. They asked me if our feast was paid for from police funds!'

'It was on the house. The place belonged to Audibert's brother-in-law. But nobody would dare charge the police such prices, the bulk of which, if I recollect the wines, would be for the drinks...'

When coffee and brandy had been served, the party reluctantly turned to the business in hand.

Littlejohn briefly outlined the case and produced the sketch of the fat man who had vanished in the sea.

'We hadn't an official *Identikit* available, but a young photographer on one of the island newspapers has made a very good attempt from descriptions received.'

Floret carefully studied the picture.

'It is extremely good if your artist hadn't seen the subject. I know the man. He is Ambroise Garnier, the brother-in-law of the murdered woman. He lives in Evian. A very eminent man, as all the members of the Garnier family were. Madame Garnier's husband, Edouard Garnier, was one-time professor of Physics at Grenoble. Ambroise was a doctor, and formerly a Professor of Surgery at Marseilles. After the war, he entered into practice at Evian. And he has vanished?'

'Yes. So far, we don't know whether he is alive or dead. To continue; I gathered that Madame Garnier also had a sister-in-law in Evian.'

Floret smiled as though recollecting something.

'Yes. Aimée Vaud. When Samson Vaud's wife ran away with an oil millionaire, Aimée took up residence with Samson. She also became known as Madame Vaud. Then Vaud died. It is all so long since that nobody but the police know they were never married. What does it matter? They were happy together.'

'What made the family all gather in Evian and live there?'

'That, Superintendent, is an easy one. Their mother, Madelon Delaronde-Garnier was a native of these parts, who married a Burgundian, went to live in Burgundy and then returned to Evian during the war. Her three sons were prominent members of the French Underground. Should any of them have been on the run, Evian was an extraordinarily convenient place to make for. You see, just across the lake was Lausanne, on neutral Swiss soil. Madame Delaronde-Garnier set up a sort of refuge and forwarding house for patriots anxious to get out of the country when the Gestapo were on their heels. After the war, her family gathered round her again. She was a local heroine for the whole town knew what she had done. Her sons joined her in Evian. It was one of the pleasantest places imaginable in which to recover from the strains and hazards after the war ended. Edouard Garnier, husband of the Madame Garnier who was recently shot in your Isle of Man, had been killed in the war. There still remained of the family Ambroise and Frédéric. Ambroise, you say has just been lost at sea. Frédéric is still in Evian, a lawyer. He is a member of the local bar, Maître Frédéric Garnier.'

'Madame Delaronde-Garnier is dead?'

'She died in 1962, from an overdose of sleeping tablets.'

'Suicide?'

'Without a doubt. She had been failing for some time. She had passed her eightieth birthday and finally became confined to bed for most of the day. She had been a very active woman and doubtless the situation palled on her. The case was one of obvious suicide. No reason for thinking otherwise. The family accepted the verdict as reasonable.'

'How did Professor Edouard Garnier meet his death?'

'That is a different matter, Superintendent. He was shot by the Germans at a lakeside village not far from here, one night when he was putting out in a boat for Switzerland. He and his comrades of the Grenoble Underground had been disturbed whilst dynamiting a train, a running fight followed in which most of the troop was wiped out. Edouard escaped with a flesh wound and by devious secret routes made his way to his mother's home in Evian. He laid low for a while and then attempted the crossing to neutral territory. The *boche* was waiting for him and shot him dead.'

'Had he been betrayed?'

'It may have been so. Nobody ever got to the bottom of it. His mother always insisted that he had been betrayed, but never said by whom. His brother Ambroise, the doctor, who was with the Resistance here in the Haute Savoie, met Edouard now and then when some big *coup* was being discussed. Ambroise declined to believe in the idea of betrayal. He said that the Vichy police and the German Gestapo had both been reinforced by first-class men familiar with the terrain of Savoy and the Grande Chartreuse and it was only a matter of time before the whole Resistance around

Grenoble and this district were either rounded-up, destroyed or flushed-out to flee farther afield. I know all this because I was with Ambroise in the local Underground.'

'And his mother didn't agree?'

'No. She was, of course, terribly upset by the death of her son. Betrayal was in the air in those days. Every setback or death in the Underground was betrayal. In my view, Monsieur Ambroise was right.'

Night was falling and it was obvious that little more could be done until the next day. Floret had booked rooms for his three companions in a country hotel high on the hillside above Evian and the lake. He drove them there.

'Would you care to come and meet Maître Garnier before I leave you, now that you are comfortably installed in the hotel? I know him well and frequently meet him in court. He occupies a flat not far from here and his sister, Aimée, keeps house for him. If you can call it that. She is, in my view, a sponger, who lives on his good nature. You could then make an arrangement to interview him tomorrow, without my being present. I have a lot of routine work to deal with and would not ask you to wait until I can get here again.'

It was agreed. They took the highway down to the town again. The last of the daylight was still hanging over the mountains to the West. Evian and the lakeside resorts were lit-up and strings of lights festooned along the promenade shone like necklaces and cast reflections on the water.

Floret pulled up at a tall luxury block of flats set in gardens in a tree-lined avenue from which the whole of the town and much of the lake were visible.

A maid answered the door and when Floret made himself known to her, admitted them at once. The hall was large and well-lighted, and decorated with exotic plants growing in tubs, pots and troughs enclosed in wrought iron. A small fountain rose from a marble basin and flung its water up and down with a splash. A large aquarium illuminated and heated, held a lot of nervous tropical fish. It resembled a synthetic jungle.

A door to the left opened and a plump little grey-haired woman with malicious dark eyes, a round face and a pouting mouth arrived. She was heavily made-up and her finger-nails were painted scarlet. She seemed to be fighting a losing battle with her weight, for, in her expensive black frock, she had the pot-bound appearance of a luscious plant struggling for space in which to grow.

She seemed to think the maid was entertaining admirers.

'Who are these men, Chantal?'

Chantal, a bright little brunette with all the appearance and charm her mistress had for ever lost, spoke peevishly, like a card player trumping her opponent's ace.

'Police.'

The elder woman's appearance changed. They might have now become long lost relatives.

'Do come in.'

She made gestures of welcome with fluent fat hands. Floret was still the spokesman.

'Pardon our intrusion at this late hour, Madame Vaud...'

'Tut, tut. Not at all. I don't know why you are here, Inspector, but I am sure it will be nothing unpleasant again. The awful death of my sister-in-law and the uncertain fate of my brother Ambroise, have made it impossible for us to bear any more trouble and sorrow. Is it about that?'

'Yes, madame. Could we speak to your brother if he's at home?'

'He is in his study. He is working. There is so much crime in the world nowadays and he is required to defend so many malefactors... I don't know how he finds the time for it all...'

One of the largest of the fish in the aquarium regarded her sadly and then emitted two large bubbles from his pouting mouth, as though trying to express his opinion in pantomime.

'Could we...?'

'I will tell my brother you are here… There's no need for you to hang about, Chantal. I will attend to our visitors myself.'

She rounded them up in the large room she had left when they arrived. It was also expensively furnished in lavish style, with a huge curtained window which overlooked the town and the lake. Modern incomprehensible pictures on the walls. An open box of chocolates on a fine mahogany table along with some novels and a tray of coffee cups. Easy chairs, plenty of cushions. And more plants. Gardenias, bougainvilleas, camellias and other romantic and passionate varieties, all in bloom.

'Please be seated and comfortable, messieurs, and serve yourselves with drinks. I won't be a moment.'

As she left, she managed to get a word to Floret privately out of the corner of her mouth.

'Who is the gentleman with the white beard? A clergyman?'

'The Archdeacon of a place called the Isle of Man, in England, madame. I think he writes detective stories.'

She gave him a blank look and shrugged her shoulders.

'I don't understand a word of what you're talking about.'

Floret looked uncomfortably at the drinks after she had left them. They were displayed on a beautiful wrought-iron sideboard, with glass panels in the cupboards and a fine top of thick greenish glass. It was like another aquarium filled with more appetising things than fish. Bottles of all kinds inside and out. Glasses of every shape and size, too. Floret hesitated to disturb the orderly pattern of the contents. He hadn't time to consider it further, for the door opened again and a man with long white hands waved Madame Vaud before him and then appeared wearing dinner-clothes with a fabulous red velvet smoking-jacket.

But it wasn't his clothes which surprised them, it was his physical appearance.

Judging from descriptions, he wasn't as tall as his brother, who had somehow got lost in the Isle of Man. He was perhaps a couple of inches smaller.

Frédéric Garnier's face, however, was startlingly like the one of the sketch now lying in Littlejohn's inside pocket. He limped slightly and carried a black cane with a golden knob and his left cheek was gashed from the corner of the eye to the jawbone by a long livid scar.

10

THE DISTRESSED LAWYER

The following morning was sunny and bright with a faint early mist over the lake.

Dorange, full, as usual, with boundless energy, awoke Littlejohn early and took him for a row on the lake before breakfast, just to show him a panoramic view of Evian, he said, from some distance across the water.

In the morning sunlight the place looked very attractive. The long, tree-lined quay and promenade, the massed flowers in the English Garden, the massive casino, thermal establishment and town hall, and the country at the back rising beyond the town terraces gently to the distant Alps. It was too pleasant to work.

When they reached land again the holidaymakers were just beginning to stir. A steady stream of elderly people, many of them invalids and some propelled in bath-chairs, on their way to take the waters of the pump-rooms. Trippers off for a long day by coach. Visitors in light attire settling down to read their morning papers on the seats along the long elegant promenade.

Littlejohn and Dorange joined the Archdeacon for a late breakfast. Then the three of them called at the office of Maître Frédéric Garnier for an eleven o'clock appointment.

The lawyer's chambers were sumptuous and contemporary. The large windows of his study overlooked the lake on the other side of which Lausanne was now coming into view as the haze lifted. The room was light and airy and the furnishings in yellow leather and light mahogany resembled more those of a lounge in a hotel-de-luxe. More modern pictures, more flowers scattered about in expensive glass vases, more semi-tropical plants, more exotic fish swimming around in a large opulent aquarium.

The lawyer was waiting for them, casually dictating to a typist who resembled a model for *haute couture* and who left them without a word when they entered, like a figure from a toymaker's shop in a ballet.

Maître Garnier shook hands all round and then set about preparing drinks with fastidious care in a silver shaker. He didn't even invite them to partake, but poured out iced dry Martini for each and handed it silently across. The only sign he gave of questioning their preference was the raising of an eyebrow as he approached the Archdeacon, who signalled with a nod that he approved.

'This is the only drink on a morning like this, Monseigneur,' he said as he handed it out.

He composed himself at his large desk and huddled down in his padded swivel chair, after placing a box of English cigarettes on a side table and inviting them to help themselves.

The Archdeacon asked to be allowed to smoke his pipe and took it and his pouch from his coat-tails.

Littlejohn guessed that Maître Garnier must be blessed with a good practice and a lot of wealthy clients to be as comfortable as this.

The lawyer screwed a thin monocle in the eye which had miraculously been spared from the damage done to the cheek below it. This disfigurement had been wrought by the Gestapo in a courageous incident which he never mentioned.

He sat back like a judge about to sum-up and pass judgement.

'Now gentlemen. I am gratified to think that the police of the Isle of Man have proved so energetic in the matter of investigating the murder of my sister-in-law and have been good enough not only to engage the services of a famous detective from Scotland Yard but also of an eminent member of our French Sûreté...'

He waved his hand in the direction of Littlejohn and Dorange, like a lecturer indicating specimens to a class of students and then gave them a small bow each.

'I trust your efforts will be successful, gentlemen. The disappearance of my brother, however, is even more baffling. Is Ambroise dead, or is he not?'

He flung out his hands and raised his eyebrows without dislodging the monocle which seemed to have become a part of his anatomy.

'Perhaps I had better begin at the beginning, sir. Our conversation of late last night was rather cursory and disjointed.'

'Do so, Superintendent Littlejohn. Do so, by all means. If you prefer you may speak English, albeit your French is excellent.'

'I'd prefer to continue in French, if you don't mind. The Archdeacon is a fluent French scholar himself and although my friend Inspector Dorange speaks English, I think it will be better for the record if we stick to his own language.'

'Please proceed.'

He helped himself to another cigarette and so did Dorange. Littlejohn lit his own pipe and then gave Garnier a brief but ample report of the whole casino affair up to the disappearance of his brother. As Littlejohn unfolded the story, the lawyer made one or two notes on his desk pad with a gold pencil, and when the account came to an end, he could hardly wait to make comments.

He was obviously disgusted with the idea that his sister-in-law should have resorted to professional gambling as a means of making a living.

'It was simply preposterous! I know my brother Edouard had lost all he had through his activities during the war, but when war ended and he was dead, there was no need for Sylvie to traipse from casino to casino to collect an income. The family would have provided for her. But she was too proud. I also see that you mentioned some kind of occult method by which she won considerable sums regularly. I have heard of it. You had better speak with my sister, Madame Vaud, about it. My sister and my brother, Ambroise, were both interested and sympathetic concerning it. Me… I am a lawyer and I believe in common sense not hocus pocus. So, as Ambroise isn't here to talk with you, there remains my sister, who is superstitious and gullible and will doubtless take much pleasure in discussing occult roulette…'

The Archdeacon looked ready to take him on about it, but puffed his pipe heavily and refrained.

'Also, I can quite understand my sister-in-law visiting the Isle of Man, where I gather, gambling is allowed and there is a casino. It would naturally be in Sylvie's itinerary of globe-trotting and roulette. But what was my brother doing there? Do you know?'

'Not yet, sir.'

'Well. I do. Sylvie sent for him. Does that surprise you? It surprises me. Ambroise, who had his surgery on the promenade and lived there alone in a flat above it, received a telephone message urging him to join Sylvie in the Isle of Man. That's what he told my sister Aimée. And what did he do? He packed a bag and took the next plane from Geneva to join her. Why? He wouldn't tell Aimée. Said it was private. And, of course, he didn't consult me. Never did. I could only think Sylvie had got into trouble of some kind. In that case, she needed a lawyer, not a doctor. Unless, of course, she'd been taken ill, which she hadn't according to your report. Aimée suggested that it might have been something to do with making a fortune at roulette and she needed help to do it. Which is equally ridiculous.'

Littlejohn felt that unless he intervened, the disorderly state to which Maître Garnier had reduced the interview would continue. It was obvious that the lawyer was very distressed about the whole affair, particularly about his brother's disappearance, and wasn't quite himself.

'Had we better leave that question until I've time to investigate the matter of the telephone call from Madame Garnier to your brother...?'

The lawyer shrugged. Then he rose, served some more drinks and moved sadly over to the window and looked across the lake as though expecting his brother suddenly to swim into view.

The boat from Lausanne was approaching and hooted on her siren to wake up everybody in Evian interested in the journey.

The lawyer turned.

'Is he still alive?'

'I can't say, sir. When the excursion boat to Dublin reached the spot where the fire had occurred in the cabin cruiser which your brother had taken from Peel...'

'You're sure he actually stole the boat?'

'He not only took the boat, but drove off in Colonel Springer's car from Orrisdale Hall to the quayside at Peel. To make sure of no interference, he left the Colonel, bound and gagged, under the stairs.'

Maître Garnier thrust his hand in what remained of his hair at the back of his head and tugged it.

'But that was ridiculous! My brother was not a man of violence. Nor was he a thief. And, if the implication of your report is that Ambroise murdered his sister-in-law, Madame Garnier, for some reason, then his endeavour to escape from justice by violence, theft and arson is more ridiculous still.'

'How else can the circumstances be explained, sir?'

The lawyer looked completely at a loss and seemed to be vainly turning over various alternative theories in his mind.

'You said he had known this Colonel Springer in the past?'

'Yes. Springer told the police they had met in the Resistance during the war when Springer was parachuted to contact the Grenoble group.'

'In that case, how did my brother know that Colonel Springer was living in the Isle of Man and in what part of it?'

'According to Colonel Springer, there was some sort of old comrades' association established by the Grenoble group and a bulletin about the whereabouts of certain members was issued from time to time. The Colonel thought that your brother might have picked up his address in the Isle of Man from that.'

'Funny, I've never heard of such a publication, although, of course, I wasn't associated with the Grenoble group and Ambroise never mentioned it to me. I assume, then, that Ambroise found himself in some kind of trouble and got in contact with the Colonel for help.'

'That is our view, sir.'

'All this is very complicated, but the outstanding point in the whole confused story is that in it my brother did not behave in a manner true to his character. From the notes I have made on your own report, I gather the following are the principal points:

'One: my sister-in-law in her professional gambling tour — I can call it nothing else — visited the new casino in the Isle of Man. There something occurred which made her wish to see my brother, Ambroise, whom she liked best of our family, because he had helped her in her time of trouble, had been associated with her and her husband during their Resistance days in the Grenoble region, and also that Ambroise was more kind and *sympathique* than the rest of our family... Or so Sylvie thought.'

The lawyer cleared his throat, took a drink, removed his monocle and then screwed it back again in his eye in what must have been a more comfortable spot, and ticked off the point on his pad with his gold pencil.

'Two: Ambroise arrived in the Isle of Man, presumably very quietly, because the police didn't seem to be able to trace anybody who'd seen him travelling. He got there on the very day that Madame Garnier met her death. Nobody saw them together. The next item of information is that Sylvie is found murdered on the shore. Was she keeping a rendezvous with Ambroise? If so, who knew of it and who met her there? I'm sure… as sure as I am here alive… that my brother did not kill her. And why did Sylvie carry a gun? Surely not to use against Ambroise? If not, of whom was she afraid so much that she needed to go armed to meet him?'

The lawyer looked round for his answers, but he got none. So he continued.

'Three: On the night of the crime, Ambroise turned up at a house… I have made a dash here for the name of the place…'

'Cronk-y-Voddy…'

'Thank you. Ambroise turns up, dishevelled at the house at where you said, is assisted, because he seems injured, and then steals away when his benefactor's back is turned. Again unlike him. He next appears at the house of Colonel Springer, for the second time. The first time was when he apparently wished to make contact with the Colonel, for old time's sake, and he seems to have asked his old comrade for hospitality. This hospitality Ambroise perfidiously repays when he arrives there again by hitting the Colonel on the head, tying him up, stealing his car and his motor-boat and putting out to sea. He had either gone mad or the story is a fable. He would never, in his true senses, have done anything of the kind. Also, where was he going in the boat?'

'To Dublin it was thought whence he could take a plane home, or anywhere else he chose.'

'Instead… Point Four: The boat gets on fire, blows up, sinks, and Ambroise, or his dead body is not traced or found. Now let me tell you this. Ambroise has himself a very fast motor-boat on the lake here. Sailing and boating are his only hobbies. He is a strong swimmer and, unless a bomb had been placed in the boat which you say he stole, would certainly never have so mismanaged the engine as to get the whole boat alight, to say nothing of blowing up. Had some unforeseen mishap occurred he would have jumped overboard and swam for the nearest land. You say he was making for Dublin and the incident occurred about ten miles from the Manx coast. Ambroise was quite capable of swimming that distance. He was a large, heavy man, but still capable of such a feat.'

Maître Garnier sat back in his chair and petulantly flung down his pencil.

'What have you to say to that?'

Hitherto, the Archdeacon and Dorange had merely been observers to the interview, sitting-in as interested parties.

Now Dorange spoke.

'If I may be allowed... It is exactly like the case of Amedée Dol, of Cannes, last year.'

'And who, Inspector, was Amedée Dol?'

The lawyer raised his eyebrows and gave Dorange a look of distaste, as though Monsieur Dol were some shabby intruder or other appearing at a time when he wasn't wanted.

'He was a bank clerk who decamped with almost two hundred thousand francs of his master's money in cash and bonds and fled to Tunis. Ten miles, or so, from the shore, he fired the motor-boat which he had stolen from Cannes harbour and swam to land with his loot. He hoped his disappearance would be taken to mean that he had perished in the fire and the police enquiry would therefore be closed. Unhappily for him, he seems to have been a victim of some kind of stinging fish in the course of his swim and was dragged from the water, half-dead, by some fishermen. He was ultimately returned to Cannes...'

'You are not suggesting, I hope, that my brother knew of this case and copied it in an effort to escape justice?'

'Certainly not, Maître. I was just reminded.'

'I don't think your recollection was either relevant or decent in the circumstances, Inspector.'

Then, to show he wasn't going to continue bad-tempered about it, he passed drinks round again.

'What, may I ask is your theory, Superintendent Littlejohn?'

'I have no theory as yet, sir.'

The lawyer looked astonished. He always thought the police had a theory; whether or not it was sound didn't much matter so long as it was a theory.

'Well, I trust you'll soon have some idea of where you're hoping to go. I don't care to have this cloud hanging over my brother and our family for any longer than can be helped.'

'I can assure you, sir, that I am as anxious as you are to see daylight in the matter. There are still some problems concerning the relationship between Colonel Springer and your brother, Ambroise, which interest me. Have you ever met the Colonel?'

'No, I never heard of him before this enquiry cropped up. I take it he was an English army officer?'

'Yes. Not a regular, I gather. He earned his rank as colonel in the war. He seems to have met both your brothers in the Grenoble group. You say you know nothing of that section of the Resistance.'

'Only casually. As I told you, I was concerned with the Savoy group.'

'Do you know anyone who *was* interested?'

'Not specifically. You'd better speak with my sister, Madame Vaud. She and my sister-in-law, Sylvie, were much together between the unfortunate death of my brother, Edouard, and Sylvie's sudden absurd interest in gambling. I think Sylvie's doing the rounds of continental casinos exasperated my sister Aimée very much. I know they quarrelled about it and relations grew strained, but long before that they had been intimate and Sylvie treated Aimée as a confidante. You should speak to Aimée. Sylvie lived in a flat of her own. She was very independent, but her belongings will all be there, including diaries, papers and the effects of my brother, Edouard…'

'I will make an appointment with Madame Vaud as soon as possible.'

'Is there anything more? Please believe me when I say that my time, my advice… everything is at your disposal to help in solving this wretched affair. It has brought great grief to me. Our family has always been held in the highest esteem and the thought that two of its dearest members should have been involved in such a sordid affair and have lost their lives fills me with despair. I do hope the matter will be settled without the reputation and memory of both of them being tarnished.'

'So do I, sir. You have my deepest sympathy. May I ask you a final question about them, personally? Your brother was a doctor. Was he in practice locally?'

'Yes. He was an eminent surgeon and had a large consulting practice in the neighbourhood. He was called in to Geneva and Lausanne very often and operated at most of the great hospitals round here. That is another thing I cannot understand. It must have been something terrible or vitally urgent to make him pack a bag and fly to the Isle of Man without arranging for his practice to be cared for in his absence. As far as I can gather, he left his patients to fend for themselves or rather to fall automatically under the care of his junior colleagues at the hospitals, without even mentioning to them that he was going away for a few days. So unlike him... He was a dedicated doctor.'

'What were his duties during the war?'

'He joined the Resistance movement, as I said. He told me before he went that surgeons would be very much needed when fighting began between the Underground and the enemy. He was stationed at Grenoble most of the time. He had a kind of portable operating theatre which he used in the locality and often treated casualties of the Grenoble group there. It was dangerous work and he lost all his equipment a number of times.'

'Probably Springer met him on some of his trips to Grenoble. He was British liaison officer there, I believe. Your sister-in-law certainly didn't send for Dr Garnier for her health. It must have been something else of great importance...'

'You know, don't you, that Edouard and his wife spent most of their time in the Resistance in the Grande Chartreuse? Not in the monastery, but in the mountains between Chambéry and Grenoble. One of their great friends is still alive there. He is a father in the monastery. He'll be very old now, but, when last I heard of him, which was recently through Sylvie, with whom he still corresponds, he was very well. He might be able to help if you want more background about what went on there during the war. His name is Laurent — Father Laurent.'

'You know him, sir?'

'No. Only of him. Aimée would be able to tell you more. Ask her.'

Apparently, Maître Garnier dined at the office and his secretary arrived to remind him that it was noon and his meal was ready.

Littlejohn's party therefore left him after arranging another meeting and went for their own lunch to the casino, which, according to Dorange, had a restaurant of repute and where Floret was to meet them with the Chief of Police of Evian.

They ate another monumental meal of blue trout and tournedos dijonnaise and washed it down with Pol Roger.

11

LES CHARMETTES

The Garnier family must have been a queer lot judging from their records. These Madame Vaud seemed most eager to divulge in the interview between Littlejohn and herself that afternoon.

Madame Delaronde-Garnier, the mother of the brood, had died of an overdose of sedative. Frédéric, the lawyer, was married, but his wife and daughter, wearied of provincial life, had set up an establishment in Paris, where the daughter was a prominent artist, who worked by spraying canvases with colours through a stirrup-pump and earned an income almost equal to that of her father thereby.

Dr Ambroise, the surgeon, had, earlier in life, fallen madly in love with a magnificent Creole woman visiting Evian on holidays, and, after a tempestuous and spectacular wooing, from which her husband had hastily removed her, had remained a bachelor.

Professor Edouard Garnier had married late in life the woman who had assisted him in his researches into parapsychology during their exile in the mountains. And Aimée... Well, Aimée didn't confess much about her private life to Littlejohn. But he heard from Floret that after his wife had run away with a wealthy Venezuelan oil-magnate taking the waters at Evian, Aimée Garnier, had, without the blessing of either church or state, taken Monsieur Vaud's name and shared his bed and board for nine happy years at the end of which he had died in her arms.

'Ask me anything you like,' Aimée said to Littlejohn when she greeted him in the hall of the flat.

Dorange and the Archdeacon had gone to Grenoble and the Grande Chartreuse to talk with Father Laurent, a Carthusian monk who had ministered to the Grenoble resistance group during the war.

There seemed to be so many leads cropping-up in the neighbourhood that the party decided to indulge in a division of labour. Littlejohn in Evian, Dorange to seek out Father Laurent in the monastery of the Grande Chartreuse and the Archdeacon, who had never visited Grenoble and the neighbourhood, to go on an excursion there with Dorange.

The fathers of the Carthusian order lived in isolation and rarely left their cells. Dorange was, however, able through his colleagues in Grenoble, to obtain permission for himself and the Archdeacon to visit Father Laurent. The endorsement of this request by the Archdeacon of Man himself did much to smooth out any ecclesiastical difficulties about the meeting.

Littlejohn's first visit after they parted was to Madame Vaud, who shared a flat with her brother in the large new luxury block *Les Charmettes,* which they had visited on the previous evening. Now in daylight the place seemed more sumptuous than ever.

There was a large courtyard to cross, surrounded by trees beneath which large cars and smaller sports models were sheltering from the hot sun. Littlejohn passed through the main doors and found himself in the hall with which he was now familiar. The porter to whom he had given his name waved him on.

'Through there.'

Chantal, the maid, met him with a smile and announced him to someone invisible within a different room from the one of the night before.

'Superintendent Littlejohn, madame.'

Another room lavishly furnished, but smaller. Presumably the private quarters of Madame Vaud. It overlooked a terrace with a garden and large trees. Beds of geraniums and begonias, roses of every description and colour and wide lawns with revolving sprays scattering water over them. In the distance, the lake.

Madame Vaud rose from a wing-chair facing the window. She was wearing a black afternoon frock with little beneath it and she welcomed Littlejohn with enthusiasm.

'Ask me anything you like.'

She must have been very good-looking in the past, but self-indulgence, perhaps to compensate for the death of Monsieur Vaud, had spoiled her figure and worried her looks. She was dark and plump and very anxious to make a good impression. She was now the eldest survivor in the family and regarded herself as the king-pin of the investigation. She was a great conversationalist and talked enthusiastically, almost with *panache*.

'My sister-in-law and I did not live together. We were individualists and of independent minds. But we saw each other every day when she was at home and there were few secrets between us.'

Although she was wearing a black frock Madame Vaud didn't give Littlejohn the impression of mourning anybody nor did she seem put-out by recent events. Her speech of greeting was said before she asked Littlejohn to take a seat. Then, after she had indicated a gilded antique chair, which Littlejohn feared might collapse under his weight, but which didn't, she rang for tea.

'You English love your tea, don't you? So do I. You've arrived just in time for *le five o'clock*. Would you care for Indian, China, or Earl Grey?'

Littlejohn said he'd go for Earl Grey which she ordered

Chantal to serve. This was accompanied by a large silver tray overflowing with iced *petits-fours* of every shape and size. These she offered to Littlejohn and then tucked into the sweetmeats through most of the interview, pausing now and then to reproach him for not eating with her.

'I feel very guilty in not making the journey to the Isle of… what was it?… Isle of Man? Yes. The Isle of Man, to claim my sister's remains and enquire about my brother, but what would be the use? He has vanished and her poor body is presumably in the medico-legal institute. So, having the comfort of knowing that the police in the Isle of Man and of London and France are skilfully investigating matters and also the very charming priest who accompanies you is giving advice on crime as well, I feel I need not interfere… My sister-in-law, did you say? When was she married to my brother? In 1943. Whilst they were in the Grande Chartreuse together. It might have been romantic in other circumstances, but they were both over fifty…'

'How did they come to be in the mountains?'

'My brother was, of course, at the University of Grenoble when war broke out. He was an atomic physicist and very eminent. When the Germans came, he joined the local Resistance in their hiding-places in the Grande Chartreuse. Sylvie, who had been a professor in the lycée at Montluçon. lost her only remaining relative, a brother, in the first months of the fighting and, being trained in nursing, she joined the Resistance, too. She was sent to Grenoble where, in the early days, the two great branches of the underground movement of Vercors and the Grande Chartreuse were centred.'

'They had, I was told, much in common.'

'You mean psychic research?'

'Was it really that?'

'Well… not exactly. They were interested in what they called extra-sensory perception from a scientific point of view. You know… telepathy, thought-reading and all that sort of thing…'

She painted it all vaguely in the air with a sugared plum which she ended by popping in her mouth.

'They had plenty of time between their plots and excursions in which to discuss and experiment. In my sister-in-law's flat at *Bel-air* there are books and books of their notes. It was mainly a kind of guessing game with cards, dice and eventually roulette wheels. I still don't know what good it did, but they seemed to be engrossed in it. My sister-in-law became an adept. She was *sympathique,* as they call it. I used to try to persuade her to foretell the future in our lives, but she said she was not a medium and found it quite impossible. She said she was only good at games. I got quite out of patience... Yet, I suppose it was something to occupy their minds during the weary days of hiding from the Germans.'

'And after much practice, your sister-in-law found she could guess the number likely to come up on the next spin of the roulette wheel?'

Madame Vaud swallowed a mouthful of candied apricot.

'More tea? No? Roulette? Yes. She couldn't somehow forecast all the numbers, but enough in a session of play to ensure her winning quite acceptable sums at the tables.'

'And she began to earn an income from it.'

'She said she was forced to do so. My brother Edouard was, like many of his kind who seem to live in theories and not in facts, a very poor financier. He used to say in his merry whimsical way that I was the best financier in the family. Many of the investments he left Sylvie proved valueless. The war, the confusion following, they made so many sources of income worthless, didn't they? I suppose you found that in England, too.'

'We did. So your sister-in-law turned to gambling.'

'Only last year, in anything like a serious way. She used to go to the casino here now and then for a little flutter to keep herself familiar with the practice she learned when Edouard was alive. She won quite nicely. But last year she went in for it more substantially. My family, of course, didn't approve at all. My brothers and I offered to ensure an income for her by creating a trust in which we would place funds. After all, a professional gambler for a sister-in-law didn't sound very good. You agree? I knew you would see my point of view. One thing we did succeed in doing. We persuaded her to leave the casino at Evian out of it. We didn't wish an exhibition or a scandal on our very doorstep.'

'So she took to touring the Continent and playing in more distant establishments.'

'Only in France. She didn't tour the world. She must have heard about the new casino in the Isle of Man and decided to investigate it. She knew England and loved it and said it would be a new experience to play roulette in public in the British Isles. A pity she didn't stay at home.'

And Aimée burst into tears, a difficult process with a mouthful of sugared nuts.

'Have you any idea, Madame Vaud, how much your sister-in-law used to win on her tours of casinos?'

Madame Vaud paused, sniffed away her tears, and considered the question. It was obvious that she was seeking a reason for knowing her sister-in-law's private business. She closed her eyes as though trying to conjure up figures and ledgers and passbooks.

'Y... e... s. When we were advised of Sylvie's death, I went to her flat to seek among her papers the wishes she may have left concerning her death and burial. My brother, Frédéric, was her lawyer, of course, but was very busy at the time...'

She cast upon Littlejohn what was supposed to be a candid, innocent look and he gave her a naïve nod in return.

'I found her bank statements among other papers. Do you know, she was so casual that she never locked a drawer or a desk. There they were. Scattered about. Papers, letters, accounts. For any servant, window-cleaner or burglar to go through. She was like that. Casual. My brother Edouard was the same. They were a good pair. Where was I? Oh, yes. At the bank Sylvie had a credit balance of about a quarter of a million francs...'

Twenty-thousand pounds! Not bad.

But Aimée didn't think so.

'...It was ridiculous. With her skill at gaming, she could have earned that in a week, instead of touring round Europe all spring and summer. She used to pay the money in a bank in the place where she won it for her credit here in Evian. Piffling little sums of five thousand francs a time. Once when she mentioned such things, I told her. Break the bank at one or two casinos, Sylvie, I said, and get it over with. Amass a million francs or so in a few weeks and settle down. But she just wouldn't see it. She said she liked going round the resorts and playing quietly and without attracting much attention. She was also able to study the places, and the other players and make a holiday of it. She said she might even write a book. I just could not persuade her to be serious. What did she want with a large hoard of money, she would say. She had no sense of money values. Nor did she realise that the faculty of ... of doing this trick at the gaming tables might suddenly leave her. She would then be poor again...'

'But you and your family had promised to come to her rescue.'

'Of course. But my chief concern, and that of my brothers, was to stop her gambling habits. It was so undignified. A Garnier earning a living by gambling. It just wasn't right.'

'Had your sister-in-law any enemies, Madame Vaud?'

'I beg your pardon. Enemies, did you say? Of course not. She was a very kind and well-beloved lady. I suppose you are wondering if anyone might wish to kill her. Put it out of your mind, Superintendent. Nobody, nobody would wish to kill Sylvie. Why should they?'

'It was a routine question.'

'Unless it was for her money. Some robber who knew she had won substantially on the tables and who killed her for her cash.'

'We are investigating that angle, but the arrival and disappearance of your brother has complicated matters a little. I believe Madame Garnier telephoned and asked him to join her at once in the Isle of Man, as something important had happened. What could that be?'

'I don't know. Ambroise didn't tell either me or Frédéric what it was all about. He simply telephoned us here to say that Sylvie had telephoned him from the Isle of Man, needed him, and he was going to join her there right away. Just that. Not a word of how, why or when. Ambroise was always very fond of Sylvie, Superintendent. He would have done anything for her. In fact, I will tell you in confidence and only because it might help you in your investigation, Ambroise would actually have married Sylvie after Edouard's death, had the family not put down its foot. My mother and Frédéric told him he *could not* do it. Not that he'd asked her, but we saw the way things were going.'

Littlejohn wondered whether or not this was before or after the affair of Ambroise and the Creole beauty of whom Floret had told him. Poor Ambroise and his amours must have kept the family quite busy.

'And that is all?'

'Everything. We still don't know why he went to the Isle of Man.'

It sounded like the popular music-hall song of long ago!

An expensive gilt clock on the marble mantelpiece struck six. Chantal came and cleared away the tea-things. And yet Littlejohn didn't feel inclined to go. Madame Vaud was a perfect fountain of information and it was obvious that the fountain didn't wish, as yet, to dry up.

'Won't you take an apéritif before you go, Superintendent. It is a great pleasure to have your company and collaborate with you.'

Littlejohn accepted and she rang for some ice and suggested they drank their *coketails,* as she called them, on the balcony over-looking the gardens and the lake.

'In our family there is only one *coketail,* iced dry Vermouth,' she said when, after considerable fuss and agitation, she finally poured out a drink. And, as her brother had said the same thing with equal pompousness earlier in the day, Littlejohn didn't argue.

They admired the view from the balcony and the beauty of the warm and balmy approach of night. Madame Vaud was showing signs of becoming sentimental and talked of the sorrows of widowhood and of loneliness. Littlejohn thought it better to get down to business again before she asked him to dinner.

'Your family must have been very brave and loyal in the war. Three brothers in the Resistance and your mother, I believe, did a lot for fugitives from the Germans.'

She pouted.

'You have forgotten *me*. My father died before the war and I was left alone with my mother when my brothers went. I, too, was of some help. I assisted my mother in most of what she did for the Resistance. In fact, she was too old to do some of the difficult physical work which I had to do for her...'

'She died some years ago, I gather.'

'Yes. The death of Edouard really broke her heart. She never recovered from it. You see, he was shot as he tried to cross the lake to Switzerland. You can see the very place from here. Down there under the lime trees. My mother always insisted he had been betrayed. He led a mission to blow-up the railway near Grenoble and the enemy were waiting for him. Only two of the party escaped. My brother and one other. The rest were massacred. We were never sure that they *were* betrayed. It might have been just bad luck that they were discovered. Edouard said they *might* have been betrayed. My mother said they *must* have been.'

'He came to Evian after that?'

'Yes. To my mother's place in the town. He hid there for one day, waiting for a dark night. Again, was it just bad luck, or had someone followed him from Grenoble, or someone here in Evian seen him and told the Gestapo? We will never know.'

'It must have been terrible for your mother.'

'I suppose you have heard that she eventually took her own

life. She could not forget Edouard. But it was made sadder still by the fact that she asked Ambroise for a sedative as she wasn't sleeping well. He didn't think when he gave her a bottle of tablets that she would take all of them. It took Ambroise a long time to get over it, although it wasn't his fault at all. She might have jumped in the lake or hanged herself, mightn't she? If she'd made up her mind she would have found a way, whatever Ambroise had done.'

She poured out more Vermouth.

'Shall I mix more, Superintendent?'

'No, thanks, Madame Vaud. I must be going. I've still a lot of work to get through and the case still awaits me in the Isle of Man. We must get back there as soon as we can.'

He took the picture of Springer from his pocket.

'Have you ever seen that man before?'

She took the sketch and scrutinised it carefully.

'No. Definitely, no. Who is it?'

'Colonel Springer, with whom your brother Ambroise stayed in the Isle of Man and whose boat he took to get away.'

'How very like the fate of Edouard. To try to escape by boat and to fail... To lose his life.'

'We're not sure he's dead yet, Madame Vaud.'

'Where is he, then? Had he been alive, he'd have been found before now.'

'We will see. I hope he's survived and is safe somewhere.'

'I feel it in my bones that he's dead...'

Madame Vaud seemed ready to work up a scene, to weep, and be comforted. Littlejohn decided it was time to go.

He excused himself and thanked her for her help and patience.

'One thing more remains. I take it the police here have taken possession of your sister's flat and sealed it?'

'That is so, Superintendent. Why?'

'I would like to go over the place sometime before I leave. Would tomorrow morning be convenient and could you meet me there at eleven? I will arrange with the police here to allow us to enter.'

She beamed.

'With great pleasure. Shall I send the car to your hotel?'

'That will be very good of you. Au'voir, then, madame.'

Afterwards, he wondered why he'd invited her, but felt there was something he still wished to know.

12

GRANDE CHARTREUSE

After lunch, Dorange, energetic and impulsive suggested that he and the Archdeacon might make the journey to the Grande Chartreuse to see Father Laurent right away.

'It's about two hundred kilometres from here — a little over a hundred and twenty miles. We should manage it there and back, with an hour to spare with Father Laurent.'

'Arriving back here about midnight, all being well?'

'Yes.'

'Right,' said the Archdeacon.

It was evident that the other three policemen thought they'd gone mad, but they said nothing, wished them *bon voyage,* and saw them off in a police car.

'Good luck... And they'll need it,' said Floret, knowing something about Dorange's furious driving. Instead of slackening speed on busy roads, the man from Nice always switched on the siren and left the rest behind.

The arrangement suited Littlejohn very well. He was anxious to get back to the Isle of Man, partly for the sake of Knell, whose condition worried him, and again, he felt that the final curtain would fall there and not in France.

The Archdeacon was eager to visit this remote retreat and to take advantage of the privilege granted to Father Laurent to break his vow of silence, to discuss other things than crime with him. Now, although used to being driven from place to place in the Isle of Man in Teddy Looney's old rattletrap at between twenty-five and thirty miles an hour, he felt the end justified the means and watched the speedometer of the police car with equanimity.

Dorange, who knew the region well, took short cuts along secondary roads as far as Annecy where they joined the main road to Chambéry through the picturesque and varying countryside and passing Aix-les-Bains and the lake of Le Bourget. At Chambéry they pressed on through Les Echelles by the road along the River Guiers to St. Laurent-du-Pont. There they slackened speed up the gorge of Guiers-Mort and penetrated into the heart of the mountain range, entered the Desert which is a prelude to the domain of the monastery of La Grande Chartreuse, and came into the lovely wooded meadows set among huge peaks, with the Grand-Som dominating them all.

The locality was a natural retreat for the men of the Resistance who held their meetings and camps there in wartime. A closed world, a vast citadel of chalk cliffs with few openings and parallel valleys ending in forests and wilderness.

It was half-past five when they arrived at the monastery and evening was already drawing-in. The austere grey buildings, relieved by six gabled towers, stood in an exquisite valley hemmed-in by mountains. There were a few cars and motor-coaches parked in the outer courtyard and the last of the tourists were busy in the shop buying souvenirs, postcards and bottles of the famous liqueur.

The Archdeacon and Dorange were expected. The Carthusian order is a silent one and visitors are not allowed in the monastery itself. On this occasion Father Laurent had been granted a dispensation and the brother who was expecting them led them to one of the thirty-six cells, each occupied by one of the Fathers. There was a small garden with each and the one they entered had three small rooms, the living quarters of which were simply furnished with a table, plain wooden chairs and a bookcase.

Father Laurent met them at the door. He was said to be very old, but, like the Archdeacon, he didn't look it. He was tall and straight, with close-cut grey hair round his tonsure, an oval healthy face, large Roman nose, bright brown eyes and a fine forehead. In spite of the discipline under which he lived, he seemed excited by the visit and his eyes sparkled humorously.

Dorange, too, seemed somewhat affected by the strangeness of the visit. Himself a Catholic, he was not only impressed by the obvious spiritual strength of the man they were visiting, but also by the almost joyful enthusiasm with which the two priests met. They made a sharp contrast with one another. The monk in his white cassock and the Archdeacon in his workaday gaiters and black suit. Two good old men, both fit and well, and glad to encounter each other.

Father Laurent, to the surprise of the visitors, said he had once visited the Isle of Man.

'A religious conference?'

'No. In my youth, I confess I rode a motor bicycle. I came to watch your T. T. races. Is that it? T. T.? I don't remember much about it, except that the sea was rough and the winner of the race averaged forty miles an hour...'

The great bell in the courtyard tolled and Father Laurent said it was time for them to be seated and discuss the business in hand.

'That finished, we can enjoy a little recreation.'

It seemed a bit out of place to bring to this peaceful spot talk of the violence and the perfidy of the world outside, but Dorange knew from the history of the priest that he was dealing with a man of the world and he made haste therefore to start the ball rolling.

'I understand, Father, that during the war, you were a member of the Underground established in the Grande Chartreuse.'

'Yes, that is right. This monastery was dissolved by a decree of the French Government in 1903 and it was not until 1940 that it was re-established. I was sent here when we resumed. Already the Resistance movement was starting all over France and these mountains, being a natural fortress, saw the founding of a section here. As the body of men who had fled to the hills grew, the need for spiritual and medical care became greatly increased. I was assigned to the groups on this side of the Isère. I visited them regularly and sometimes, I even crossed the River Isère to the Vercors...'

There was a pause and a moment of dead silence. In 1944, after a magnificent stand by the Vercors Resistance, the Germans had burnt the villages and slaughtered the inhabitants.

'You were, I believe, well-known, Father, and familiar with most of the principal figures of the local Underground...'

The priest smiled gently.

'Quite true, although they weren't very much underground. They were very lively on the surface.'

'You knew Professor Edouard Garnier and his wife?'

'Yes. I married them, in fact, whilst they were here. They were great friends of mine. I am very sorry that since we last met, they have come to such violent ends.'

'You also knew Dr Ambroise Garnier, the professor's brother.'

'Yes, though not so well. Dr Ambroise had a roving commission. He was a brilliant surgeon and whenever a case got beyond the skill of the ordinary doctors who served the Resistance, Dr Garnier was called in. He often came at the risk of his life, but never failed us.'

Dorange paused.

'And now, Father, I want to ask you some questions which might be intimate, about these personalities. If anything I ask goes beyond the seal of confession, please tell me.'

'I don't think there is any fear of that. You are a discreet officer and will know when you go too far.'

'Thank you. First of all, about the professor and his wife. Madame Garnier was, as you may know, murdered in the Isle of Man last week. The motive of the crime has, so far, eluded us. Only by building up a background of her life can we possibly come to a conclusion about who committed the crime. It may reach back to the days when she was here.'

The priest nodded.

'I follow. Let me tell you something about the Garniers and, if you wish to question me further, do so.

'Professor Garnier was a very eminent nuclear physicist and had held a chair at Grenoble before hostilities. He at once joined the local Resistance and found refuge here in the mountain retreat. He was a strange man. He and I spent a lot of time talking and arguing together in the quietness of the hills...'

He turned to the Archdeacon.

'You, my friend, know that many physicists have become interested in the supernatural. Your own Oliver Lodge, Crookes and many others, are examples. It is as though they encountered forces which their science could not explain and caused them to seek reasons in other directions. Garnier was extremely interested in para-psychology, the new science which studies phenomena outside the senses of man... That was really how he met his wife. She, a highly intelligent woman, was interested in the same thing. They spent hours and days experimenting. She, it seems, was particularly good as a subject for their experiments. She was, to a certain extent, what is termed psychic. What to many others of their colleagues in the movement were card games covering an interesting courtship, were to Garnier and his friend extremely serious almost solemn experiments. You know of all this?'

'Yes, Father, we do.'

'Then I will not bore you further with it. Now this is very important, Inspector. Professor Garnier was very far advanced in nuclear fission. He had a world-wide reputation as a nuclear scientist. You know what that meant during the war... and after. It was absolutely imperative that he should not fall into the hands of the enemy. That was an edict both from the heads of the French underground movement here and the control in London. The order went so far as to say that rather than allow him to fall in the hands of the enemy, he was to be shot.'

Outside, all was still. Dusk was falling and the last of the sunlight penetrating the valley cast long ominous shadows across the courtyard, like a setting for the story of doom which was unfolding.

'But the professor was a stubborn man. And brave, too. He refused to be penned-up in the hills and insisted on taking part in all kinds of enterprises. That was finally his undoing. He indulged in the most dangerous adventures imaginable.'

'Kindly tell us how he finally met his death.'

'In the summer of 1944, four thousand men of the Resistance under Colonel Huet engaged the enemy in harassing operations in the Vercors arising from the re-entry of the Allies in Europe. Over a number of weeks, they pinned-down enemy forces numbering five times the Resistance troops. The enemy poured in two divisions from every direction. It was then that the railway branch line from Grenoble to Villard-de-Lans became strategically very important. It was planned to blow it up in several places, particularly at a viaduct near St. Nizier-du-Moucherotte. Naturally, every available help was rushed to the Vercors and, as neighbours, the Grande Chartreuse sent men. Heading a squad to assist in the Villard demolitions, was Professor Garnier. He insisted and would not be persuaded. Either the plan was betrayed or, what is perhaps more charitable and likely, the enemy had redoubled the guards on the line. The project failed. Garnier and another comrade were the sole survivors of their particular party. And now, I must tell you of the other survivor...'

There was an interruption as one of the brothers entered

carrying a tray of bread, salad and wine. He silently laid the table and after a gesture of farewell, left them.

'You have a long journey back. Let us eat as I talk.'

And they all fell-to.

'Now about the only other survivor. I told you that strict orders had been given that Professor Garnier, who, by the way, was known by the pseudonym of Carolles — for safety's sake, the members were usually called by other than their own names — must not fall into enemy hands. The professor was headstrong and insisted on playing a practical part. It was finally decided that he should be provided with a bodyguard, a professional soldier responsible to headquarters in London. A British colonel was parachuted to us for the purpose. He was known as Grimaud.'

'You knew his real name. Father?'

'No. It was not, shall we say, etiquette to ask a man's true name and nobody found it troublesome.'

Dorange took from his pocket the sketch of Colonel Springer, made by the reporter in the Isle of Man.

'Do you recognise that man, Father?'

The priest looked hard at the picture. Then he took a reading glass from the bookcase and scrutinised it carefully again.

'This is Grimaud. Much older and with a moustache, but if I mentally shave off the moustache it is the same man.'

'Thank you. Grimaud now lives in the Isle of Man.'

'Indeed! And is he mixed-up in this crime of yours?'

It was strange that Father Laurent showed no excessive or unhealthy curiosity about the crime. He seemed interested in and content with such details as Dorange cared to give him.

'Yes, we think he might be. It is obvious that he did not suffer the same fate as Professor Garnier.'

'We knew that. Garnier and Grimaud escaped and fled across the mountains to Evian-les-Bains, where Garnier's mother lived and had been helping fugitives across the lake into neutral Switzerland. He and Grimaud stayed one night with Garnier's mother. Then, next night, made an attempt to cross Lac Léman. They were spotted by the local Vichy police, there was a fracas, and Professor Garnier was shot dead. Grimaud disappeared in the darkness. Later, we heard that he swam across in the direction of Lausanne and was picked-up and taken safely over by a customs launch. That, I think, is all I can tell you.'

'You have not met any of the parties since then, Father?'

'No. You see, shortly afterwards the enemy were slowly pulled out of these parts. There was much to be done in re-establishing our order in the monastery and I was called home. Once here, of course, I became subject to our Carthusian discipline and no visitors came to see me. Now and then, we had news. Visiting priests and others brought word of things outside. We are allowed, as you know, to speak together during our weekly walk and on Sundays.'

'What happened to Dr Ambroise Garnier after the war ended?'

'He returned to his mother's home, I believe, and took up practice in Evian. I never saw him again after the war.'

They finished their meal as the last of the daylight sank over the valley.

Then, Dorange removed himself tactfully, making an excuse that the car needed some attention.

'I'll be back in a minute or two. Doubtless you two gentlemen will find something to talk about whilst I'm away.'

He returned in quarter of an hour. The two priests had not been talking of crime, but of matters which seemed to please them more. The monk saw them to the door and bade them goodbye.

Dorange had to drive more slowly owing to the darkness until they reached the main road. Then he climbed up to his usual speed. The Archdeacon was quiet for most of the journey and Dorange did not disturb him. There had been a sense of sadness in the parting at the monastery. This had been a special occasion and they would not meet Father Laurent again.

They reached Evian at eleven o'clock.

126

13

BEL-AIR

Next morning the Archdeacon stayed late in bed and
Littlejohn and Dorange met Floret in the office of the
hospitable chief of the Evian Police. There was a full discussion of
the case and a detailed exchange of information.

Floret, who had been pursuing official enquiries arising from
the past history of the case, has secured some vital information.

'The records of the Vichy police, who controlled this region
during the Occupation, have been moved to Paris. I telephoned
there for any details they might find in the archives of the case of
Professor Garnier and his death by shooting as he attempted to
escape across the lake to Switzerland. That was in 1944.'

He referred to a memorandum he held in his hand.

'The Chief of Police of Haute Savoie and the local heads
during the Vichy régime are no longer available, as you might
expect. The chief shot himself at the Liberation and the rest are
scattered and gone. But the records, for what they are worth, have
been preserved. Shall I read the relevant parts of the routine
reports on the case? I have made a rough précis.'

'By all means do so, please.'

'Briefly, then, they are as follows:

'*September 1st, 1944.* Reported that after the discovery and frustration of a plot to demolish sections of the Grenoble-Villard-de-Lans railway, two of the leaders of the plot had escaped pursuit. Thought to be heading in direction of Swiss frontier. All stations alerted to watch Lac Leman and other borders. Military and police look-outs strengthened on the Thonon-Evian sections, craft available for crossing lake strictly supervised, likely places of refuge inspected. Suspicious persons rounded-up and questioned. No results as yet.

'*Later.* Message received from Grenoble that the two escaped men were likely to be Professor Garnier, of Grenoble, son of Madame Delaronde-Garnier, of Evian, and a British colonel seconded to the Grande Chartreuse group and going under the name of Grimaud. Madame Delaronde-Garnier interviewed. No results. Men stationed to guard and watch her residence.

'*September 4th, 1944. 22.30.* Alert from sentries at Post 4, at Le Vieux Mottay, mouth of River Dranse. Two unidentified men reported by village police seen on Evian side of delta. Surrounded by picket. Shots exchanged. One escaped and apparently entered the lake. One left dead behind. Found to be shot through the head. Abandoned rowing-boat found between scene of skirmish and the lake. Body of dead man later identified as Professor Garnier. Further investigations later.

'*September 9th, 1944.* Post mortem examination of body of Garnier, shot during fracas of September 4th at Le Vieux Mottay. Death by revolver bullet. Military and police all carried rifles or automatic guns, except village policeman who stated he fired several shots from his regulation revolver. Such shots would be ineffective as the range of the revolver too short. In any case, bullet which killed G, was not of type used by police or military. It was from a small calibre pistol of very moderate power. Examination of head led to inference that shot fired at close range. May have been killed by random bullet from other man's revolver in the dark. Intendant of Police suspended further enquiries.

'*September 9th, 1944.* Informed by our agent in Lausanne escaped British officer picked up by Swiss customs craft early morning September 5th, midway between Lausanne and Evian. Assumed to be Grimaud. Will be interned.'

Floret closed the file and handed it to Littlejohn.

'And that is that.'

'It looks as if Grimaud, or Springer, carried out his instructions to shoot Garnier rather than allow him to be taken. Springer must have been very impulsive. If he got away himself, why did he think Garnier wouldn't be able to do the same?'

'It is so long ago and the records are so sketchy, probably owing to pressure of work at the time, that we'll have difficulty in finding out much more about the affair.'

'I'm very grateful for what you *have* done, commissaire. And now, any news from Deauville?'

Floret had telephoned Deauville as being, according to the dated receipts found in her belongings, the last place where Madame Garnier had remitted funds through a bank to her account at Evian before she left for England.

Quite satisfactory. The police there visited the casino. Madame Garnier played there on three evenings before she left for the Isle of Man. The manager of the Deauville casino had jocularly mentioned to her that she'd be surprised to learn that there was now a public casino, with roulette, *chemin de fer* and the rest, open in the British Isles, in the Isle of Man. Madame Garnier said she'd never visited the Isle of Man and thought she might go.

'So that's the simple explanation of her visit to Douglas, although her sister-in-law told me she'd already read about it in a newspaper. Curiosity, and the new casino.'

'Apparently just that.'

'And now, before we keep our appointment with Madame

Vaud to inspect her late sister-in-law's flat, we've one more piece of information to wait for. News from the Isle of Man about Madame Garnier's phone-call to Dr Ambroise Garnier.'

Earlier, Littlejohn had rung Douglas police, found Knell unexpectedly back in harness and, to use Knell's own words, as fit as a fiddle again. He had asked him, if possible, to trace the call made by Madame Garnier from Douglas to Evian on the day she died and to enquire what it was all about.

They had not long to wait for the answer. Knell's familiar voice, slightly excited by success and therefore more resonant with Manx brogue, came over the distance as though he were speaking from across the promenade of Evian.

'It was a bit sticky at first, sir. The telephone girls never care to admit that they listen-in, you know. But when I pressed the matter and mentioned the casino murder, one of the girls told me that she'd dealt with the call. I promised that she wouldn't suffer by breaking the rule; quite the contrary. She said that on the day before her death, Madame Garnier at about 9.15 a.m. put through a call to Evian apparently from her room at the casino hotel. Are you there, sir?'

'Yes, Knell. You're coming over fine. What next?'

'It was to a number in Evian. A man answered. Madame Garnier said, "Is that you...?" The girl didn't catch the name. But the man answered "Yes". Then the French lady said, "This is Sylvia".'

'What was the number, Knell?'

'I got that. Excuse me a minute...'

A pause whilst Knell presumably consulted his elegant notebook.

Meanwhile, Littlejohn drew the local telephone directory lying on the desk to him and looked up Ambroise Garnier's number. Evian 843.

'Here it is, sir. Evian-les-Bains 843.'

'Splendid. Please go on. Was all this in French?'

'Yes. The telephone girl knows French very well. She said she followed the conversation, such as it was, quite easily. The message was very brief. The lady said, "I've just met…" and a name which sounded like Jumbo or Grumpo…'

'Grimaud.'

'You knew all the time?'

'No. I just guessed.'

A pause as though Knell were sorting out what Littlejohn meant.

'And then…?'

'The man answered, "Are you quite sure?" Answer: "Yes, I'm sure." And then he said, "I shall join you at once. I'll telephone you when I arrive." Then she gave him her number and rang off. There were no greetings or pleasantries exchanged. They both sounded too earnest for that, according to the telephone girl.'

'Did the man ring Madame Garnier later?'

'I tried to trace any phone call inwards to her, but none was recorded. It must have got by in the rush. The hotel's very busy.'

'Very good, Knell. A great help, thanks. Are we doing all right, did you say? Yes, making progress. When are we returning? Probably leaving tonight. We'll be in the Isle of Man by the first plane from London. Inspector Dorange, of the Nice Sûreté, is here helping us. He's on holiday, like I'm supposed to be. He's coming back to the Island with us. He's never visited the Isle of Man before and the Archdeacon has invited him to Grenaby.'

Noises of great enthusiasm about the Island and its new visitor from Knell's end.

'Just one other matter, Knell. Last, but by no means least. I take it you've kept a careful watch on the man at whose house you recently suffered considerable damage? No names. You understand?'

'I get you, sir. Yes. There's a night and day tag on him and the house.'

In case there was someone listening on the line, no mention was made of Springer by name.

'It's most important he doesn't disappear. I want to see him as soon as we're back again.'

'I'll see to it, sir. After what happened to me, I want a word or two with the same person.'

'Well, we'll see you soon.'

Littlejohn had, in view of pressure of business, sent a message to Madame Vaud that he would meet her at her sister's flat and she need not, therefore, call at his hotel with her car.

When he arrived with Floret, Dorange and the Archdeacon, Madame Vaud looked surprised and annoyed, she'd been anticipating a *tête-à-tête*.

Madame Garnier's flat was in the large converted mansion of Bel-air standing in the best part of the town and in its own fine garden. Madame Vaud was waiting for them at the door. They climbed three steps and found themselves in a wide, square hall, with a lift on one side serving the upper floors. Madame Garnier's rooms were on the ground floor.

Madame Vaud led them along a corridor to the door, which had already been sealed by the local police. Floret broke the seals and they entered a large sitting-room the shutters of which were closed. Floret opened the largest window and thrust back the shutters. There was a magnificent view of the lake beyond the garden.

There were three rooms; a salon, a bedroom, a spare room, and a small kitchen. The place was sparsely furnished, but each article of furniture was tasteful and expensive. Madame Garnier had obviously been a tidy woman and nothing of a hoarder. The place was clean and well-kept, books were arranged in orderly cases, the drawers were neat and seemed to contain nothing superfluous. There was, under the window, a writing-desk, the drawers of which contained stationery and a few bills and papers of a formal nature and quite without interest. Through the open window they could hear the birds singing in the garden. Some-where, an unseen gardener was raking the gravel and there were gusts of noise from the busy town below. There was a large well-kept flower-bed under the window and the faint scent of old roses wafted in.

Madame Vaud sat in an empire armchair, lit a cigarette, and waited for developments.

'You'll not find anything of interest in this room. The drawers are full of furnishings of various kinds...'

She meant table linen, cutlery, glass and china apparently, for that, they found, was mainly what came to light.

The second room, a spare one, had been a kind of boudoir, with a couple of wardrobes containing clothes, and a dressing-table the cupboards of which mainly held cosmetics and medi-cines of various kinds.

There were two tallboys in the bedroom. They contained clothing too. A large bed with a carved headboard set in an alcove. But the room was dominated by an exquisite empire bureau the drawers of which, unlike those of the rest of the furniture, were locked.

The policemen carefully and gently went through all the unlocked drawers, found nothing helpful and then returned to the bureau in the bedroom. Madame Vaud rose and followed them.

'I'm sorry but my sister-in-law had the key for the bureau and her effects haven't yet been returned. I suppose they'll arrive with the body. So, it seems you will have to wait.'

Dorange, who had been very busy making a rapid examination of the place, smiled.

'That should present no difficulty, madame. Allow me.'

He took from his pocket a small object known as a *rossignol* to French criminals, turned his back on the assembled company and made one or two rolling gestures with his shoulders. All the drawers stood open.

'You need not fear, madame. I'll lock them all again when we have finished.'

Three drawers contained little of interest in the case. A cash-box with a small amount of money in it; a small account-book; pass-sheets, cheque books and a receipt for a certain amount of jewellery deposited in the bank for safety; a small investment register covering a fair number of bonds and shares...

Madame Vaud must have found a key somewhere to fit the bureau, for she had already given Littlejohn details of money matters contained in the locked drawers. She gave Littlejohn a questioning sideways glance, but he said nothing. No use creating a diversion now. Neither did she explain why the masses of diaries, letters and papers with which she had said the place was crammed, were nowhere to be found. Perhaps Madame Garnier had disposed of them rather than have Mme. Vaud rifle them in her frequent absences.

Throughout, it gave the impression that Madame Garnier had cut herself off from the past and had merely been living in the present.

During the inspection of the whole place, Littlejohn was impressed by the fact that nowhere was there any trace, memento, photograph or picture of the late Professor Garnier. No papers or letters of his; not a thing. Not even a book bearing his name or dealing with the subjects in which he had specialised.

Had Madame Garnier found his tragic death too much to contemplate or the memory of him too bitter to bear? Or, had their relations towards the end of his life deteriorated to such an extent that she wished to obliterate all memory of him?

The bottom drawer of the bureau contained simply a locked strong-box which Dorange opened nimbly with another small tool from his pocket collection.

'What is that?' said Madame Vaud. 'More money?'

Dorange placed the box on the table and they gathered round as he flung back the lid.

It contained a flat gold cigarette-case with the monogram of Edouard Garnier engraved in a panel on the front. Dorange pressed the edge and the case flew open. It held four cigarettes which crackled with age as Dorange squeezed them with his fingers. On the inside of the lid had been stuck a head and shoulders snapshot of a woman, dark, young and beautiful, with close-cropped hair and wearing a blouse which might have been part of a uniform. It could have been taken in strong sun, for she seemed to be having some difficulty in facing the light... It was signed *'Toujours. Alice.'*

Madame Vaud breathed heavily.

'Who is that?'

'You didn't know her?'

'Certainly not. That was Edouard's case which my mother gave him. As for Alice... Well... It's just ridiculous. Edouard? He wasn't that sort. Carrying pictures of strange women around with him. There must be some mistake.'

There was only one other thing remaining in the box. A foolscap envelope without address. Dorange slid in two fingers and took out a sheet of soiled paper, apparently a piece of a notebook.

Alice Faure,
23 bis, Rue de la Solitude.

It was written in the same hand as that of the inscription on the photograph.

Floret took the slip of paper and examined it carefully.

'Rue de la Solitude. That's in Lausanne. Excuse me... I'll just...'

There was a telephone in the sitting-room and Floret hurried out, dialled and asked for a number. Then there was a rapid conversation. He returned to join the rest in the bedroom.

'I've rung Lausanne police and enquired about anybody called

Alice Faure. We are good friends and keep in touch. There will be a short delay.'

Madame Vaud couldn't get over the idea of her brother carrying a photograph of a strange woman about with him in his cigarette case.

'There must be some mistake. Edouard wasn't that sort...'

'Whilst we wait for a reply to Inspector Floret's enquiry, could you tell me something of your brother Ambroise during the war? Was he in the Resistance, did you say?'

'Ambroise? Of course, but he didn't take to the mountains. He was, at the time, a practising surgeon in Grenoble. Very eminent. He served the various groups of the Resistance, though, and whenever needed, either through wounds or illness, always answered the call. Often at great risk to himself. Had he been caught... Well... I shudder to think... He sometimes visited my mother here in Evian, during the war. But he was kept very busy. Is that what you wish to know?'

'Did he and your brother Edouard meet frequently during the war?'

'Yes. The Chartreuse group was nearest to where Ambroise lived; he sought out Edouard now and then and sometimes was called out to his group in an emergency.'

'And, at the end of the war, Dr Ambroise returned here and quietly resumed his normal routine?'

'Yes. Very many brave men did that, didn't they?'

'Yes. I would like to thank you for helping us in our business in your late sister-in-law's flat. It must have been very distressing to you. She never confided in you about anything that might be connected with the cigarette case and the note we have discovered?'

'No. This is the first I have known of it. It came as a great shock. What does it mean?'

'I'm sorry, I've no idea, but we must find out...'

The telephone rang in the next room and Floret hurried out to answer it. There was a long conversation and then he returned.

'The Lausanne police were easily able to trace the lady in question in their old files. September 1944.'

There was an air of tension, almost *malaise* in the room.

'She occupied a small flat in Rue de la Solitude. She seems to have rarely been at home. But, in September 1944, she was found dead in the flat; shot. There was no evidence of any description to show why or who had done it. Either Alice Faure had kept no records or even clothing in her flat, or else the murderer had cleared out the lot. Nobody saw anyone enter the flat. The neighbours in the building didn't even know that Alice Faure had returned. It was all a mystery and never solved. She was killed by a small bullet from a .25 automatic pistol at close range. The weapon was never found.'

'No papers?'

'Yes. A French passport was found in a drawer of the room. That was all…'

'Had the Lausanne police any theories about the crime?'

'Oh, yes. During the war, with access across the lake and nearby frontiers so comparatively easy, all kinds of international conflicts and mysteries were regularly occurring. The death of Alice Faure was true to pattern.'

'Why?'

'The Lausanne police kept a watchful eye on doubtful characters and Alice was one of them. They knew her and her record. She was an agent of the Vichy police.'

1 4

LAWYER'S CONFESSIONS

Maître Frédéric Garnier was most effusive when Littlejohn called on him a second time. Instead of ringing the bell and ordering his attractive secretary to usher his visitor in, he himself walked into the waiting-room, made purring noises, shook the Superintendent by the hand and helped him into his private office by placing his arm around Littlejohn's shoulders and gently propelling him.

Then there was the usual routine of the iced Vermouth, the only 'coketail' worth drinking.

At length, they got down to business. Maître Garnier screwed his monocle in his eye to show he was listening.

'The main purpose of my call, sir, is to say good-bye and thank you for your help and hospitality…'

The Garnier family had insisted on paying the hotel expenses of their three visitors. 'It concerns the family and its honour and we insist that you be our guests.'

'…We are returning to the Isle of Man by the early plane from Geneva tomorrow.'

The lawyer nodded his head sadly, as though grieved to lose them all.

'Have you arrived at a solution of my poor sister-in-law's death already? If so, I would be interested to know the results. After all, it is a Garnier matter.'

'I'm sorry, sir, but we haven't got so far yet. We have gathered some very useful information here which will help us wind up the case when we arrive back. But there is still work to do at the scene of the crime.'

'I realise that. I hope you will let me know as soon as you have arrested the culprit. Have you yet had any news of my brother? That's what concerns me most. I take it, his body has not been found and there is no news of his landing in Ireland. What am I to think?'

'We are as much in the dark as you are, Maître. The local police are diligently pursuing every line. That is as far as I can go. You will be kept informed.'

'Your visit to *Bel-air*... As my sister-in-law's advocate, I was formally asked for permission for the police to enter and search the flat, although they had already impounded and sealed it. Did anything come of the search?'

The lawyer took out a cigarette, lit it, and passed a cigar box across to Littlejohn, who, however, filled and lit his pipe.

'That brings me to a number of matters about which I would like your opinion. Were you aware that your brother, Edouard, had a mistress?'

Maître Garnier took out his monocle, polished it, replaced it and smiled indulgently.

'You are a man of the world, Superintendent. You understand these things. Edouard was not immune from the weakness of his kind. He had an eye for a pretty girl.'

'This doesn't seem to have been a passing fancy, sir. It involved his honour and, had he not met his death when he did, perhaps his complete ruin.'

'My dear Superintendent! You must not dramatise the matter. Who was this woman?'

'During our search at *Bel-air* an hour ago, the only item of interest in our case was found in a locked box in a locked drawer. It was a gold cigarette case, in which was fastened a snapshot of a young lady. In an envelope in the same box, was her address in Lausanne. Did you ever hear of Alice Faure?'

The lawyer began to look uneasy for the first time. He tried to pass it off with a show of irritation.

'My God! Has that old affair been revived! I heard enough about her after my brother's death to last a lifetime. It seems she was a Vichy spy, who had been insinuated in the Chartreuse group and, it was thought, may have been responsible for the failure of the railway *coup* which ended in the death of the whole party, except my brother and one other man. At any rate, she was found murdered in Lausanne a few days after the event, so, it seems the Resistance had followed her when she fled and seen justice done.'

And he sat back, uncomfortably waiting for what he knew was coming next.

'Your brother, Edouard, seems to have been very intimate with her. Her photograph in his cigarette-case and her address in his papers. They suggest close relationships and perhaps a rendezvous over the border.'

Maître Garnier thumped the desk.

'My brother died honourably. I will not have ill said of him when he isn't able to defend himself. How can what happened so long ago affect your present investigation?'

'One, perhaps two of your family, including your other brother have been killed through something which happened in the events of 1944 which we are discussing. I am quite sure of that.'

'In what way?'

'I must ask you, Maître, kindly to let me ask the questions. I wish to know exactly how much you know of the events of the night of September 4th, 1944. The night your brother Edouard died.'

'Very little. I'm afraid I can be of no help.'

Littlejohn didn't seem to have heard.

'After the failure of the Grenoble railway plot, your brother came to Evian?'

'Yes.'

'Where were you at the time?'

'Here. I was one of the Resistance, but it was thought that, in my position, I could help more by staying where I was and continuing my practice.'

'And your brother Dr Ambroise?'

'In Grenoble.'

'Was your sister-in-law, Madame Garnier, still in the Chartreuse with the group?'

'No. She had not been well and returned to my mother's home for a time.'

'How did she manage to do that? Wasn't she, as well as her husband, known to be a very active member of the Resistance and therefore on the black list with a price on her head?'

'That is so. My mother, however, was also connected with the Resistance and frequently gave secret hospitality to fugitives from the police and the Gestapo. There were hiding-places in her house. My brother sent his wife to his mother because he feared her illness — it was nervous — might jeopardise the safety of the rest of the group.'

'Might it have been, Maître, that your brother's attitude towards his wife had changed through his relations with Alice Faure and had caused the nervous strain you mention...'

The lawyer struggled to his feet, livid with rage, and pointed to the door.

'I think you had better go. You don't seem aware that you are now discussing members of my family who died honourably for their cause. I resent your questions and your dragging them into the case.'

'Please calm yourself, sir. We have no intention of making all this public. It is past history. But I must know all I can about the events of 1944. Otherwise the murderer of your sister-in-law and possibly of your brother, may escape scot-free.'

The lawyer slumped in his chair again.

'Please excuse me. These matters are most painful to me. One catastrophe after another. First my brother Edouard; then my mother. She killed herself out of grief eventually. And now, two more of the family. It's almost more than I can bear. It all rests on my shoulders. There's only Aimée of the family left besides me. And Aimée is a fool...'

'I'm very sorry and I won't trouble you more than I can help, Maître. What happened after your brother Edouard's death? There was an enquiry, I suppose.'

'Yes. Officially, of course, our family fell under a cloud. To have a brother caught openly helping the Resistance was a crime in itself. But this region was a very loyal one to France during the occupation and the Vichy régime. Our friends didn't desert us. The end of the war and Liberation were not far away in 1944. Our friends here sustained us. None of us was arrested. Even in Grenoble, my brother carried on in practice. Sylvie, my sister-in-law, managed to stay here, hidden and helped by many friends until the Liberation set her free.'

'Did she occupy the flat at *Bel-air* in those days?'

'It remained the property of herself and my brother, but they rarely occupied it. We suspected it was under surveillance, you see.'

'At one period, then, Professor Garnier and his wife were under your mother's roof together. I mean, they would meet as the professor was in flight and on his way to the border.'

'That was so. Yes.'

'Were they friends then?'

The lawyer looked surprised.

'What do you mean… friends?'

'To be quite frank, sir, Madame Garnier must have known of the relationship between her husband and Alice Faure.'

'Oh, I see. I don't know. I wasn't there. It was thought best that Edouard and I shouldn't be… well, shouldn't meet. I might have been followed, you see.'

'To return to the matter of the enquiry. Did you ever know the result?'

'No. Our family were snubbed by the police. We received no information whatever. The Prefect, an old friend of mine, managed to arrange for the body to be buried in our family vault and we attended the funeral. The coffin was not opened. After the Liberation, I had the body disinterred and Ambroise, my brother, identified it. That was all.'

'So you didn't know how he died, except that he had been shot in trying to escape from Evian.'

'That is so.'

'We have had the old Vichy records turned up in Paris. Your brother was not killed by a bullet from a rifle or regulation firearm. He died from a shot at close quarters from a small calibre pistol of very moderate fire power.'

'His companion, the second man, shot him?'

'His companion was an English colonel, did you know?'

'Yes, I learned all about him from my brother Ambroise. So, rather than let my brother fall into enemy hands, the Englishman shot him.'

'I don't think so. Grimaud was an army man. He would be armed with a *real* revolver or pistol, not with what was almost a toy.'

'Who did it then?'

Littlejohn thrust his hand in his pocket and took out the gun found in Madame Garnier's bag in Douglas.

'Have you ever seen that gun before?'

Maître Garnier gingerly picked up the weapon, dropped it and recoiled.

'It belonged to my brother, Edouard. Where did you find it? At *Bel-air?*'

'No, in the Isle of Man. It is the gun which killed Madame Garnier. In my view, it killed your brother and Alice Faure. too. We will soon know. Before I came here, the local police fired two shots with it and the bullets have been sent across to Lausanne for comparison with the one still in the files there, which killed Alice Faure.'

'There must be some mistake. That gun... I haven't seen it since the war. Edouard took it with him when he joined the Resistance. I knew that because when he came to bid me good-bye, he asked me if I'd any cartridges which would fit it. He had only a small supply. I had a gun of my own which he knew about. We tried my cartridges but they wouldn't fit Edouard's weapon...'

'Where is your gun, now, sir?'

'That's just the point, Superintendent. I lent it to Sylvie about six months ago. She had taken to making these trips to various casinos and sometimes had considerable sums of money in her possession, her winnings. I couldn't persuade her to give up her roulette playing and begged her to take care. There are so many violent people about nowadays. I insisted she take my gun with her. I never used it. She knew how to handle such things from her Resistance days. She said to put my mind at rest, she would carry my gun and she took it and put it in her handbag. That's the last I saw of it.'

'And she said nothing about the gun I've just showed you?'

'No, except that I asked her before I offered mine to her if she hadn't kept Edouard's pistol. She said no. It had disappeared either during their time in the Grande Chartreuse or during his last journey. Perhaps the local police had taken it when they found his body. At any rate, she had never seen it since the days they were in the mountains.'

'Your gun was not in your sister-in-law's possession when her dead body was found in Douglas. Instead, her late husband's gun was found in her bag, hidden in some bushes near the beach.'

The lawyer rose and staggered to the cabinet at which he dispensed his 'coketails' and opened it. It was brandy this time and plenty of it. With his customary good manners, he didn't forget Littlejohn in his plight. He half-filled a balloon glass and handed it to the Superintendent. Both of them felt better after a quiet drink.

'And now, sir, do you feel inclined to tell me all you know?'

The lawyer sat back. He seemed to have recovered his confidence. He gave Littlejohn a straight look. Now that he had dropped his professional mask and guile, Littlejohn liked him.

'You and your Anglo-French team, Superintendent, have done a marvellous job. In strictest confidence within, of course, the needs of your duty, I will tell you what occurred. Mind you, I am not able to give you information as though I were on the spot. This which I'm going to tell you was from Sylvie, Madame Edouard Garnier. My mother suspected that Sylvie killed Edouard. She saw her follow him out on the night of his death and saw her return later. She knew that Edouard had betrayed both his wife and his country and, although the relations between her and Sylvie were never the same again, my mother seemed to keep her thoughts to herself and never mentioned it. I think she had managed to forgive Sylvie before she died. You see, Edouard had become infatuated with Alice Faure. It must be said that until it was too late, he didn't know she was a Vichy spy. In fact, it was only after the Grenoble débâcle that it dawned on him. Alice fled, leaving him with her address in Lausanne.'

Garnier took another drink and lit a cigarette with trembling fingers.

'The rest is only surmise. He had certainly betrayed Sylvie

most abominably. He must have fallen in love with the young and beautiful Alice and more or less cast Sylvie off. She was in a terrible state when she arrived at my mother's home. She told us everything, including that she was sure no good would come of it as it would lead to betrayal. She had an instinct, she said. My mother and I put it down to jealousy. It must have been more than that. News arrived from across the lake in Lausanne, that a suspected woman spy had been found shot in Lausanne. Just a few lines in a journal which we sometimes imported to get news of the world around. There was a picture of her. One of those terrible things taken of the corpse after dressing it up decently. It was, Sylvie said, Alice Faure. Sylvie had seen her picture in Edouard's cigarette case, which she had removed from his coat before he left my mother's on the night he died.'

'And did Sylvie confess to murdering Alice Faure, too?'

'No. We didn't even ask her. But if Edouard's gun proves to have been the weapon, Sylvie must have crossed to Lausanne and taken revenge. There were ways of getting across, even in those difficult times, if you had the money. Sylvie must have disposed of the gun afterwards.'

'And you have carried this secret with you all this time, sir?'

The lawyer sighed and took another drink.

'As a lawyer, I'm used to such things, but when it came to my own brother and his wife and murder, I found it hard. Especially after my mother died, and I was left alone with it and the thought that my mother's suicide was due to her mind breaking down under the burden of family guilt. Aimée, of course, didn't know anything about it. Had she done so, it would have been a secret no longer.'

'And that is all, sir?'

'My God! Isn't it enough?'

Maître Garnier splashed out more drinks in the glasses. He might have thought that Littlejohn was referring to the brandy!

'And now, Littlejohn, it's your turn to confide in me. What happened to Sylvie in the Isle of Man?'

It was a funny thing, but questions of that type always reminded Littlejohn of comic songs. And of Florrie Forde. What happened to Sylvie in the Isle of Man!

'I still don't know. But what I do know, sir, is that Grimaud, the man who fled from Grenoble with your brother, who was commissioned to take care of his safety and kill him rather than allow him, with his knowledge of atomic science, to fall in enemy hands, and who probably both saw your brother killed and who his killer was, is now living in retirement in the Isle of Man. He and Sylvie may have met. Who knows? Why did she send hurriedly for your brother, Dr Ambroise? And what happened when the doctor got there? Those are questions we haven't yet found answers for. I hope we soon will find them.'

'So do I. Could it be that Grimaud tried blackmailing Sylvie about something when he encountered her? He might have seen her shoot Edouard and threatened to tell the whole story.'

'It's quite possible. We'll have to see. I'll keep you informed, sir.'

They parted amicably and Littlejohn made his way on foot to join his friends.

The sun was shining and the lake was gay and busy with small craft and trim lake steamers. As he looked across at Lausanne, he imagined the grim scene in 1944, with every way out watched by loyalists, traitors and the friends and enemies of France.

He halted in his stride as a thought struck him. Then he hurried on to his rendezvous.

Floret was there waiting with the rest.

'Yet another piece of tedious investigation, Floret. Can you find out from records, or even by digging up someone who was with the Vichy police and survived, if possible, whether or not the Grenoble railway affair and the proposed flight of Garnier to Switzerland were betrayed to the authorities and by whom?'

'That may not be so difficult. We had, I believe, a patriot posted in the Thonon Sûreté, who passed on all important news to the Resistance headquarters there. He is pretty old now; around eighty. But he's lively enough. He lives with his daughter. We'll go and consult him. Care to come and meet him?'

15

AN OLD WARRIOR

R obert Lansard, retired caretaker of the Thonon police station, lived at Rives, the lakeside village port for Thonon-les-Bains. The detectives left the car in the town square and descended by the funicular to the port.

It was a hot afternoon and the thin heat haze over the lake obscured the Jura mountains on the opposite shore. Around the little port all the coloured awnings and sunblinds were out, children and young swimmers were sporting in the lake, and groups of men and women sat drinking under the gaudy umbrellas erected over the outdoor tables of the cafés. The boat to Geneva was just arriving and blew a blast on her siren.

Floret and Littlejohn strolled along the quayside, resisting the temptation to stop at one of the cafés and cool-off over a glass of beer. Floret led the way to a narrow street which turned at right-angles to the quay and slowly petered out as it climbed the slope to the upper town.

The street contained a motley assortment of dwellings. To celebrate the holiday season, many of them had been given a new coat of paint and their fronts shone in red, blue, white and grey indiscriminately. The bulk of them were cottages with here and there a shop or a café. One of the larger ones was a wine merchant's. Finally, the cottages thinned out and left spare plots of land dotted here and there with shanties and allotments, most of them half neglected and lavish in overgrown vegetables, as though their owners had succumbed to the heat and the holiday season and decided to leave them to their own devices.

There were very few people about; the heat had either driven them to the shade of indoors or to the cool drinks of some café or other. Most of the doors were open and in the gloomy light cast by the small windows they could see the occupants engaged about their business. A woman mopping a floor, a man sprawled across a chair with his feet on the table and a cigarette in the corner of his mouth, reading the paper, an old woman sitting on a wooden chair in a doorway, making lace. In many of the dwellings the radio was going, churning out the same accordion solo from door after door.

Littlejohn, charmed by the locality and always interested in out-of-the-way railways, lifts and funiculars, had himself suggested that they leave the car in the upper town and travel the rest on foot. Now he was beginning to regret it. The hot still air met them in waves, the heat of the pavement struck through his shoes and made his feet hot and dry and the sun seemed to penetrate the nape of his neck and skull and fuddle his brain.

Just before the street changed to a path which penetrated the trees of the hillside stood a shabby bistro and a small house. Three scruffy youths in narrow light-blue trousers and stripped to the waist, were lolling at an iron table in front of the café drinking Coca-Cola from bottles. Their hair was long and greasy and they stared insolently at the newcomers, with the aggressive irony of local riff-raff for towny visitors.

The end house consisted merely of a single storey and was made of concrete blocks roughly thrown together. There was a small neat garden in front and a narrow path leading to a freshly painted green door, which stood open. Floret knocked and waited. Dead silence.

They entered. A large half kitchen, half living-room with a small bed in one corner hidden under a coloured quilt. The place was neat and clean, with an iron cooking stove at one end, a sink, and a round rough table, covered with a blue plastic cloth, on which stood a bunch of half-faded marigolds in a glass vase. A sideboard covered in odds and ends of souvenirs and ornaments with photographs in cheap frames scattered among them.

'Anybody at home?'

The only other room seemed to be behind a closed door on the right. This door now opened and a woman emerged. She had a dark, tired face and the tight hard lips of one who was having a struggle to make ends meet. The newcomers had their backs to the light and she peered hard in an effort to recognise them.

'What do you want?'

And then almost in the same breath,

'Is it you, Inspector Floret?'

Her voice and attitude changed and her face relaxed. She must have been handsome until struggling for existence and worry had aged her before her time. She seemed around fifty, but might have been younger.

They could hear movements and the creak of a bed in the room behind her and a man's voice called out.

'Who's there, Maxine?'

'Inspector Floret and another gentleman, Dad.'

'Bring them in.'

Before she answered she whispered to Floret.

'His bad leg's started to bother him again and the doctor's put him to bed. He's afraid of gangrene...'

Lansard had fought on the Marne in the first war and received a bad wound in the leg.

Maxine drove them before her into the bedroom. All very neat and clean and completely dominated by a large walnut bed topped by a massive green quilt. Whitewashed walls with a few religious colour-prints hanging from nails and a Medaille Militaire reposing on a pad of red silk and enclosed in a small case with a glass front. The room was full of tobacco smoke.

An elderly man — he was around eighty but he didn't look his age — was sitting up in bed surrounded by newspapers and paper-backed novelettes. He was smoking a pipe. Clean, shaved, and with a large moustache of the old military type, he received his visitors with great respect. He and Floret seemed on the best of terms.

'Well, Robert, and how goes it?'

'Please excuse me, monsieur le commissaire, for not being on my feet to welcome you. The doctor and my daughter have been fussing again and Maxine has hidden my trousers and my boots...'

'Quite right, too.'

'I am sorry to find you taking sides with the enemy, monsieur le commissaire.'

Floret introduced Littlejohn. Lansard said he was honoured by the visit.

'Maxine! Bring the bottle of *fine* and some glasses, my girl...'

She hurried in with the brandy and poured them out a tot each.

'Pour one for yourself, too, my girl.'

They drank one another's health before getting down to business. Lansard said he remembered very well the Grenoble affair in 1944 and the flight of Professor Garnier to Evian and his death there.

'I was on duty at the police station that night. They brought in the body and put it in the morgue and I remember there was a real schemozzle because he hadn't any papers on him. The Sub-Prefect was there in person and said somebody had taken them from the body.'

'Was there anything else left in the pockets?'

'No, sir. There was another fugitive with the professor and it was assumed that he had taken away anything by which the body could be identified. Which was stupid, because the professor was a very well-known man locally. Anybody would have recognised him.'

Maxine fluttered in and out, removing the papers and books on the bed, tidying the room, watering a geranium blooming on the window-sill.

'Please excuse the state of my room, gentlemen. I have nothing to do all day at present, except read papers and tales and shuffle about in the bed... You were saying...?'

'Do you recollect the day when news came through to the police and military that the Grenoble railway *coup* had been discovered and had failed and that it was thought certain fugitives were travelling in this direction?'

'Certainly I do, sir.'

'Who took the message?'

'I did, sir. My main job had been to clean and generally take care of the police premises and the kitchen there, but as the force became fully extended and occupied through the efforts of the Resistance, I was told I'd have to look after the telephone switch-board, as well. I was quite willing. It meant overtime without extra pay but it suited me and my friends. You see, I, too, was in the Resistance. I was very useful even in my humble job, picking up bits and pieces here and there. An odd remark, a piece of paper in the waste basket when I emptied it. I soon learned the use of the switchboard. I used to listen-in to messages whenever I could without giving myself away. Once or twice I thought my number was up, but I just played stupid and got away with it. I am a simple sort of man, messieurs, and I expect the authorities thought I was too ignorant to be of much use to the Underground, even if I knew that such a body existed...'

Lansard was enjoying the visit to the full. He could have gone on, talking, talking, talking for ever.

'Excuse me, Robert, but did you intercept any messages about the fugitives, particularly about Professor Garnier when he was being pursued?'

'I was coming to that, Monsieur Floret. I did. Information about the affair was so important that, instead of being passed from one police post to another, it came direct from the Prefect's office in Annecy to the Sub-Prefecture here. The Sub-Prefect spoke to the chief of police himself and told him he wanted the fugitives, or else… The message came through my switchboard. It was of little importance. We knew already through the local Underground that the professor and his English comrade were on the way here. When the message arrived from the Sub-Prefecture, I could have told them where they could have found the two fugitives. They had gone to the professor's mother's home. Old Madame Garnier's place was an old house at the end of what is now the Quai Paul-Léger, in Evian. It had been in her family for generations and she had removed back to it on the outbreak of war. It had once been a headquarters for smuggling contraband across the lake and there is still a secret cellar in it where the contraband was stored. The professor and his friend stayed there for one night only. The military had searched it and the commander threatened to blow it up if the two men were not found. It was thought advisable to get them away quickly. The result of the haste was disaster.'

To prevent their being cast-down by old news, Lansard called for the brandy again.

'You will take some more, messieurs. You will already know that it is the real thing. My brother-in-law sends me some now and then. He lives in the Charente…'

More glasses, more good-healths, more compliments. The old boy was doing his best to spin-out the visit.

'The message from the Prefect? It was nothing. It led them nowhere. No. It was the message sent direct to the police station here from someone local that did the damage. I shan't forget that night till the day I die. I was there, at the police station, tidying-

DEATH SPINS THE WHEEL

up, ready to turn over the switch to my relief. It was about eight o'clock. The buzzer went on the telephone board and I answered it. Someone was asking for the chief of police and nobody else would do...'

Another sip of brandy to keep up the tension.

Lansard wiped his copious moustache with the back of his hand.

'The chief was there. They'd been grilling a suspect somebody had brought in and he'd been working overtime at it. I put through the call. And, as it seemed important, I left the switch open and listened in. What I heard made me go hot and cold, I can tell you.'

Littlejohn's mind was working in two directions at once. He was fully aware of the tale unfolding and completely interested, and yet his eyes kept wandering in the direction of the geranium on the window-sill. It reminded him of the Archdeacon's new conservatory and he wondered how it was getting along! Grenaby seemed far off in another world just now.

'...A man's voice, it was. He gave no name, although the chief tried every way he could to find out. It simply said, "The two men you want are crossing the lake from Le Vieux Mottay later tonight" and then whoever it was hung up. It was all over in a few seconds, otherwise, if I'd known, I'd have disconnected the line, whatever trouble it caused me. I didn't know what to do. My relief had arrived, so I picked up my things, bade him good night and casually made for the door. I wished to get a message through about what had happened. Instead, the chief appeared at the door of his room. "You're on duty all night, Lansard," he says to me. "Get back to the switch. Your relief man will be needed else-where." I was helpless. There was another officer in the room with me on station duty. He seemed to suspect what I wanted to do and his eyes never left me. If I tell you that they shot him at the Liber-ation, you'll know how I was fixed. You know what happened, messieurs...'

'The voice of the traitor, Robert… A man's?'

'Yes. Disguised, too. He spoke in his beard or else through a cloth over the instrument. I couldn't recognise it.'

'You said it was a local call?'

'Yes… Evian, I'd say. Mind you, that's only a guess. But when one works on the switch day-in day-out for a long time, one gets to recognise the little peculiarities of the various lines. For instance, I knew that the Thonon internal lines were quite clear that night. I'd had several local calls. On the other hand, we'd had trouble with the line from Evian all day, because, knowing there were fugitives in the district, the Resistance in the locality had been destroying as many communications as possible and had cut the Evian telephone lines in four places in the day. Temporary repairs had been made, but the lines were still poor when the message about the professor leaving came in. I knew it was from the Evian section.'

'You'd no idea who might have called the police?'

'No, monsieur. With the bad line and the obvious efforts to disguise his voice made by the caller… But I will say, it was an educated voice. No hesitation for a word, even if he only spoke briefly. The chief, however, in his usual clever way, said he'd recognise it again. But that was like him. He knew everything.'

'All the same, did he say *why* he'd recognise it?'

'He was showing-off over the phone later, speaking to the Sub-Prefect. He said he'd swear the informant was Burgundian by the way he rolled his R's. I was listening-in at the switch the morning after when they were discussing it. The Sub-Prefect laughed and said Burgundy wasn't the only place where they rolled their R's. Which was right. I could have told them that. But the chief got excited and said he'd go so far as to guess the place, as he himself had lived in Burgundy till he was seventeen. As there was no chance the informant would give himself up just to settle their argument, the matter was dropped.'

'What part of Burgundy did the chief come from?' 'Let me see.

I've seen it in the files somewhere... Lucysur-Yonne, that was it. He'd a sister there and it was at her home that they found him after the Liberation. He was spending a quiet holiday there.'

'And there's nothing more that you think might help us, Robert?'

Lansard levered himself higher in his bed, as though it might somehow help his memory.

'I suppose you know all the sorry story of the railway affair at Grenoble and how and why it was a failure. The group was betrayed.'

'Yes, we have the file on it all. Alice Faure was insinuated in the group as a spy and Professor Garnier seemed to become infatuated with her. They had arranged to meet in Lausanne after his escape. Instead, he was killed and she was later shot, too, in Lausanne, presumably an execution for her perfidy...'

'But that couldn't have been all, sir, could it? Who was the man who betrayed the professor to the Vichy police here? And why did he do it? It had been hinted, you know, that it was the professor's wife who arranged for him to be betrayed and the police tipped-off about him. That, on account of his letting both her and the Resistance down. Did you know he wasn't killed by a bullet from a service rifle or pistol? It was a small bore gun, what you'd call a private little weapon, not a wartime weapon at all. Did you know?'

'Yes, Robert, we knew.'

Littlejohn thought that it would have been a good idea and the saving of a lot of time if they'd visited Robert Lansard earlier in the case. He seemed to know all about it.

'Have you any views of your own on the matter, Robert?' he asked him.

Lansard's face lit-up. It seemed he'd been waiting for this.

'I've given the matter a lot of thought, sir, especially when my leg's bothered me and I've had to lie-up in bed or been kept awake at night by it. I look at it this way. I don't know much about these

159

scientific matters, but I do know that Professor Garnier was a clever scientist who, it's been said more than once, was well on the way to making a weapon which might have ended the war earlier and made possible a complete defeat of the enemy. The enemy were trying either to kill him, or capture him and make use of his brains for their own purposes. They sent this Faure woman to get the secret from him or else capture his fancy and get him to cross into enemy territory. Since the war ended and the Liberation came, we've learned that, at the same time, there was an English colonel, sent by the de Gaulle faction in London to see that no harm came to the professor or his ideas. If we look at all the possible people who could have shot him, we think of the English colonel. And we cross him off the list because he'd never have used a toy pistol to shoot Professor Garnier and keep him out of enemy hands. He'd have made sure and used a service weapon, a sure killer. Would I be right?'

'Yes.'

'That leaves the Faure woman, who might have shot him because she knew he couldn't get out France and might still use his invention against her side. But, unless she accompanied the professor, she wouldn't have been there to do the shooting. She was, from all accounts, waiting for the professor to join her in Lausanne when she was killed. That seems to leave Madame Garnier, his wife, to do the job. The weapon was the sort a woman would own. I think she did it. Found out that the Faure woman was his mistress and that they'd a rendezvous across the lake when he'd escaped. She knew his plans, because he must have told his mother when he was hiding there. My guess is that it was his wife who did it. And if what I heard was true, she was justified.'

He paused and his eyes sparkled as though he was about to give them a treat.

'There's still one mystery about it all I never solved.'

'What is it, Robert?'

'I was always intrigued about what the chief of police said

about the voice on the telephone that betrayed the whereabouts of Professor Garnier. The chief, his name was Rolland, won a bad reputation throwing in his hand with Vichy, but he was no fool. In fact, I always found that whatever he said during an enquiry was worth taking notice of. Well, I remembered what he said about the informant being Burgundian on account of rolling his Rs. I made a few enquiries here and there about who might have come from that part of France. There were a few families, but somehow, I couldn't see how they could be linked with that telephone call. Then, one day, somebody was talking about the professor and just by chance remarked that the Garnier family originally came from Clamecy on the Yonne.'

'You mean…?'

'Madame Garnier, the mother, was an Evian lady, but the father was a prominent man in Clamecy, in Burgundy. The family were brought up there. I pursued my enquiries a bit further. There were four children in the family. The professor, Monsieur Edouard; the lawyer, Maître Frédéric; the doctor, Monsieur Ambroise; and the sister Madame Aimée. Of the men, Maître Frédéric, the barrister, had completely lost his Burgundian speech, owing, I suppose, to his public speaking. But the professor and his brother Ambroise were both proud of their Burgundian origins and never quite lost their local accent…'

He paused and shook his head, puzzled.

'The professor was hardly likely to betray himself, was he? So Dr Ambroise was the only one left of the family who might have telephoned. He was fanatically loyal to the Resistance. I wonder if when he heard of his brother and Alice Faure… All the same, I knew Dr Ambroise well. He wouldn't kill a fly. During the war, his work was entirely in saving, not killing people. He gave his talents as a surgeon entirely to France.'

'So that eliminates them all, Robert?'

'Yes, monsieur. And it leads me to one theory only. The family of Garnier were closely questioned at the enquiry into the professor's death. It was ascertained that he was armed with a small pistol, his own property, which he had owned before the war and still carried. It was of the type which matched the bullet which killed him. It's my view that the authorities here finally decided that Professor Garnier killed himself rather than fall into the hands of the Gestapo. And that the gun with which he shot himself got lost in the swamp of the river delta. But the authorities here did not make that theory public. Oh dear, no. They'd have looked silly and incompetent letting the man they wanted so badly get away like that. So, they let it be known he'd been shot by the military whilst trying to escape.'

16

STRANGER IN FLESHWICK BAY

Floret had promised to send a police car to take Littlejohn, the Archdeacon and Dorange to Geneva airport to catch the 13.45 to London and arrived promptly, driving himself and obviously excited. He bounded up the hotel steps, three at a time, and made for Littlejohn right away. The travellers were enjoying a final drink in the lounge before departing.

'I have some good news for you, Superintendent. Just before I left, your comrade Knell...'

He pronounced the usually silent K in the Inspector's name very emphatically.

'...Your comrade Knell telephoned. Dr Ambroise Garnier has been found and is safe and well in the Isle of Man.'

It was one of those strokes of good luck which, now and then, seemed to enliven Knell's existence.

The Island police had, with the help of coastguards and fishermen, diligently searched everywhere, without success, for traces of the man known as Allasac.

Then, early one morning, the policeman at Port Erin, a pleasant little summer resort on the western side of the extreme southern tip of the Island, had called in the chemist's shop there.

He had a painful ulcer on his gum and wanted something to relieve it. The young lady in the shop supplied him with a remedy which she promised would do the trick.

'Anything fresh?' asked P.C. Quinney — locally pronounced 'Cunyah' — for want of any other conversation.

'Nothing much. Old Mr Quate has gone to hospital for an operation and Arthur Kinnish took the tip off his finger on the bandsaw. Oh... and Miss Redpath's dog fell over the cliffs at Fleshwick and broke a leg and tore his side open. It must have been pretty bad; she took a big parcel of dressings away. She said she climbed down the cliffs and rescued him herself. A tough sort of woman.'

Quinney thought nothing more about it, until he reached the police station where he lived. He halted on the steps. Then he hurried indoors to his little office and consulted his records of licences.

Miss Redpath had never taken out a dog licence.

The constable put on his helmet again and got out his motor-bike.

Miss Redpath was somewhat of a recluse who occupied an old, white-washed isolated crofter's cottage on the hillside above Fleshwick Bay. She had arrived in the Isle of Man after the war, bought the house, renovated it and settled there. She didn't welcome visitors and spent her time working and digging in the small garden which surrounded the house. Her past was something of a mystery, but it was known that, during the war, she had been interned in France by the Germans. She now earned a living by writing, nobody quite knew what, and by translating foreign works into English.

Quinney made his way slowly along the narrow country road which led to Fleshwick. He was doubtful about what his move should be when he arrived at his destination. He could ask for the dog licence and might be merely interviewed at the door and sent about his business. To his way of thinking, that would not be enough. Recent instructions from headquarters had urged the closest observation and investigation of any unusual incidents or visitors to all localities in the Island and the following-up of suspicious events or behaviour. A description had been issued of the missing Frenchman and all personnel had been told to be on the look-out. It had even been hinted that the man known as Allasac had not left the Island, but might be in hiding or even lying dead in some remote spot.

Quinney had reached the quiet Fleshwick valley, set deep in the hills and which suddenly opens out in a pretty little bay with a stony beach. A place very popular with excursionists, but deserted for most of the time. Miss Red-path's cottage stood well away from the motor road to the bay, accessible by a rough path closed by a gate. From the front door of the house, the whole magnificent countryside and the main road were visible.

The front door of the cottage was open when Quinney turned the corner. He halted and dismounted from his bike and hid himself under the tall hedge to ponder on his strategy again. He finally decided to take the place by storm and come upon the occupants unaware before they had time to plan their defence. He didn't know who he'd find at home. Probably nobody but Miss Redpath. In which case, he'd ask to see the dog and politely book her for being without a licence for it. If the Frenchman was there, he'd have to ask for an explanation. He took the photographic copy of Perrick's synthetic picture of Allasac from his tunic pocket and studied the details again, just in case.

Quinney very cautiously approached the gate from the main road and unfastened it. With as little fuss as possible, he slowly swung it open. Then, he returned for his motor-bicycle, mounted it, and rushed at full speed up the path like a desperate T. T. racer on the last lap. Right to the open front door. As he dismounted, happy to find that there had been no apparent resistance, there was a movement inside and the door was slammed shut. Quinney swore to himself and almost ran the rest of the way. He beat on the panels with the flat of his hand.

'What do you want?'

A woman's voice, hoarse with either emotion or sore throat.

'This is the police madam. It's about your dog licence.'

'Go away. It isn't convenient for me to discuss it now.'

'Do you keep a dog?'

'I said it wasn't convenient...'

Her voice tailed away as another, this time it sounded like a man's to Quinney, seemed to be arguing with her. The exchange of views took quite a long time and the bobby began to wonder if he were being the object of some trick or other. He slapped the door again.

'Open in the Queen's name!'

He had said it before he realised what he was doing. He vaguely wondered if he'd done right. Was it legal and proper to use such a sacred and high-sounding Open Sesame in the circumstances and what would be the result? He stared at the door as though expecting it to crumble to powder or the roof to fall in. Instead, the door opened.

'Come in.'

Miss Redpath stood there. Quinney was quite surprised. Hitherto, he'd seen her only in the distance. At close quarters she was quite handsome, although her look of resignation now had turned down the corners of her mouth sadly. She was tall, dark, and with traces of grey in her dark hair. Her face was tanned by the sun and clever looking. She wore a homespun frock which didn't improve her good figure. She had grey eyes which she fixed on Quinney to his discomfiture. He felt that if he hadn't found a sudden ally in the unknown second occupant of the cottage, she might have been a very formidable adversary.

'Come in.'

Quinney had known the cottage well in days before it was converted. It had once been occupied by a poacher with whom he'd tried conclusions a time or two. Now, it was completely transformed from the dump he'd once known. A wide window admitted plenty of light and air, the walls had been colourwashed in pastel shades and the furniture was cosy and attractive. There were some good etchings and watercolours on the walls and shelves crammed with books.

But Quinney had only time to take-in the general atmosphere of the place and admire the change briefly. For, half lying on a couch under the window, with his leg up, was a man whom Quinney recognised right away. It was Allasac.

There was a pause and then the two occupants started to speak fluent French to one another. Quinney felt like he used to do when his grandparents spoke Manx together and left him out in the cold.

'I'd be much obliged, madam, if English could be spoken, if you please.'

The man seemed to understand what it was all about and apologised.

'I had no intention of being discourteous...'

The woman appeared to enjoy Quinney's awkwardness now that the Frenchman seemed at ease.

'You were asking about the dog, officer?'

'If you don't mind, madam, we'll leave that minor matter over for the time being. May I ask the name of your guest? Is it Mr Allasac, alias Ambroise Garnier?'

The man replied.

'That is so, officer. I cannot say that I am at your disposal, as I have a broken leg and third degree burns on much of my body. So you'll forgive me if I don't stand when I speak to you.'

'That's all right, sir. But I must inform you that the police have been searching for you for several days and I shall have to ask you...'

He was going to say, 'accompany me to the police station', but he realised that he'd have to change his tack.

167

'...I shall have to ask you to remain where you are until I can contact the Inspector in charge of the investigation. Are you on the telephone, madam?'

'I'm sorry, I'm not, constable. The farm across the valley have one. If you care to go there and speak to your superior officers, I'm sure they will let you do so...'

The man on the couch had been following the conversation and spoke up.

'You need not be afraid to leave us whilst you telephone, officer. I had intended calling on you at the police station as soon as possible. I have only been waiting until I could walk properly. Had I sent you a message, you would only have had me removed to hospital under guard. I felt it would be much pleasanter here...'

He spoke good English with a decided French accent and, as he mentioned his preference, cast a sly sideways look at his hostess.

'I cannot walk yet and, in any case, I give you my word I will remain here until you return. I would be the last person to wish to cause Miss Redpath any embarrassment. You have been most courteous and considerate in the circumstances. I ask you now to do me this last favour.'

'Of course. If I have your word, sir. I'll leave you while I phone then.'

Quinney had a good idea of men and how much they could be trusted and he knew that this time he was backing the right horse.

'I'll not be long.'

He wasn't. He was back in ten minutes, glowing with the congratulations which Knell had heaped upon him.

There were tea and scones waiting for him when he got back. When Knell and another policeman arrived, the three of them, Miss Redpath, Dr Garnier and Quinney were sitting over the teacups, chatting like old friends. Quinney effected introductions all round.

Knell was rather at a loss. He couldn't arrest Garnier for

murder, until Littlejohn returned with the missing pieces of the enquiry. He was one of those persons who in official jargon, were sought by the police to help them with a case.

'I'm sorry to find you in such poor condition, doctor,' Knell said with his usual politeness.

Dr Garnier smiled at him.

'But I'm not in poor condition, Inspector. On the contrary. My injuries are healing splendidly and Miss Redpath has been feeding me like a fighting cock, as you say. I shall soon be able to call at the police station in person and tell you my story.'

'I'm sorry, sir, but that won't do. I gather that, with the help of Miss Redpath, you have been treating yourself… I mean doctoring yourself. You know better than I do what condition you're in. Can you say you are fit for a long talk with me?'

'I think so. Miss Redpath and I, during my stay here, have had many long talks. No reason why you and I should not do the same. What do you wish to know?'

'What happened to you after you took Colonel Springer's boat and fled to Ireland in it?'

Miss Redpath emerged with more tea and scones and offered them to Knell and his constable.

'Thank you very much, Miss Redpath…'

Knell drank his tea and then excused himself whilst he made for the nearby farm again to telephone. He felt he must let Littlejohn know at once that Allasac had been found. For weeks afterwards, the wonder of the rapid connection between his farm and France and the subject of the ensuing report was the sole topic of the farmer's conversation. When Knell returned, they resumed their talk.

'You mentioned my taking Colonel Springer's boat, Inspector. It was the other way round, I'm afraid. The boat took *me*. I was unconscious from a blow on the base of the skull when I was placed in the boat and my course set for… Well, I assume actually it was for Ireland, although Springer intended I should end up in heaven or hell. I was put in the boat unconscious. Not tied-up, of course. That wouldn't have done. I was placed in the boat, the wheel was set, the engine started, and off I went at high speed out to sea. The method of my death was quite simple. The deck soaked in petrol, two more open cans at a safe distance from the engine so that we wouldn't go up before our time, and a simple device to make a spark and ignite the lot in due course.'

'Which it did?'

'Yes. I had been laid below in the engine pit. I recovered too soon. We were far enough at sea, but I was supposed to go up, not to swim. It was some time before I realised where I was or what was happening. Then, I acted as quickly as my fuddled brain would allow. But not quickly enough. The time device that fired the petrol went off. I was a mass of flames right away. The only salvation was to jump in the sea. As I did so, I was so unsteady that I caught my leg in the rail and broke my tibia and fibula, the former a compound fracture. Thanks to my own knowledge and Miss Redpath's skill, we have dealt with all my injuries, although I must confess the after-care of my leg will require hospital treatment. We made our own plaster for the leg, but the ingredients and other necessities, such as bandages, had to be obtained elsewhere by stealth. To allay suspicion in the town, we invented a dog with broken bones and other injuries. I'm afraid that wasn't clever enough for your excellent constable, Quinney.'

'What happened when you dived overboard, sir?'

Knell was treating the man on the couch with increasing respect. Stretched out as he was, he seemed huge. In spite of his plight he was well-groomed, poised, polite and obviously anxious to help. He spoke slowly, pausing now and then for the right word, but conveying his meaning with obvious ease.

'I dived into a nightmare, but not as bad as the one I had left. The boat was ablaze from stem to stern and finally exploded and went up in what seemed to be hundreds of pieces. I am, thank goodness, a very strong swimmer. I must have struck out mechanically and the buoyancy of the water prevented much pain in my damaged leg, although I could not use it. I was aware that the burns were bad, for my clothes were stuck to my body. And yet, the water seemed to ease the pain there, too. It was the blow on the head which Springer gave me which troubled me. I was still only partly conscious and had no sense of direction. Luckily, it was a clear day and I could see land. It was this island and I made for it again.'

'You didn't see any of the boats which came searching for you?'

'No, not near the spot where the explosion occurred. Now and then, I saw ships passing far away, but soon I seemed to lapse into unconsciousness. I must have still made swimming strokes, for I found myself near land eventually. As soon as I felt the solid earth, I must have fainted with the pain of my injuries as the water drained away and the air circulated freely about them. I remember waking to find Miss Redpath giving me the kiss of life. It was dusk then. She had been gathering driftwood. I fell in the right hands, by the mercy of heaven. It took hours, it seemed, to get me to this place, but once here, we started treatment, and you see me as I now am. Unable to walk much but recovered from the worst of my burns, although they are far from right. Miss Redpath wished me to call in another doctor, but I knew that would mean hospital right away. After I had told her my story, she agreed with me that I had better stay here for a time. I am. after all, a surgeon myself, and considered myself in safe hands.'

'We thought you had perished with the boat, sir, but continued to search. Meanwhile, our friend Superintendent Littlejohn, of Scotland Yard, is in Evian exploring the French angle of the case. I went to report your being found to him over the telephone. He will inform your family and he is returning to the Isle of Man today.'

'We will see what he has found out in Evian. I wish to God I were back there. I've had quite enough of trying to be the law. I much prefer medicine. Will that be all, Inspector?'

'I'm sorry, sir, but it won't. I hope you are fit to continue this interview.'

'I am. But let it be as short as possible, please. It is almost lunchtime and your island air and Miss Redpath's cooking have made me hungry. What can I tell you?'

'Why did you come here, in the first place, sir?'

'Now, that is a long story, Inspector, which will take a long time...'

Miss Redpath intervened.

'You must not tire him. Although he seems full of energy, he is still far from well. It will be weeks before he is fit even to walk a little. There is bound to be a reaction after the excitement of this visit. I haven't enough in the larder to invite you all to lunch, but there is enough for one more. If the two constables could dine elsewhere, you, Inspector Knell, might join the doctor and me in a meal. No, no. I insist. The doctor can talk quietly with you over the meal. It will be mere ham and eggs and I am sure that judging from the unusual amount of food I have bought over the last few days, it might easily have been the grocer, as well as the chemist, who set Constable Quinney on our trail. Where was I? The two constables... Would the pair of you mind foraging elsewhere?'

The pair of them said yes, they would. In fact, other duties called them. So, after Knell had arranged for them to return in an hour or so, they left the other three to their meal.

Grace Redpath set the table alongside Garnier's couch and there they sat down together. The whole interview had developed on such amicable and helpful lines that it was only after the meal had arrived that Knell realised that it was a rather funny affair to be indulging in ham and eggs with a pair who had already technically broken the law and who might, if matters developed that way, find themselves on the other side of the fence from the police and charged with greater crimes than hiding an important witness.

Nevertheless, the atmosphere remained cordial and the conversation went on in friendly fashion.

'And you, Miss Redpath, why didn't you inform the police about the half-drowned man you found on Fleshwick beach?'

She looked him quite candidly in the face.

'I didn't know who he was until after I'd given him a promise not to disclose that he was here. In any event, I was far too busy dealing with my patient, tidying him up and seeing to his broken leg and scorched chest to be running all over the place advertising that I'd rescued him and was harbouring him here...'

She paused and then added gravely:

'Besides, it gave me a chance to repay the French something of what I owe them. In 1940, I was a governess in Caen when the Germans poured into France. A last boat was sent to collect the English residents there and take them home to England. Somehow, I was forgotten, left behind, and then interned in a stinking prison in Bezançon for more than eighteen months. When I was released, I was dressed in a costume, if such you could call it, made from a potato sack and I was a mere skeleton. Had I been compelled to stay there until the end of the war, I would have died. But a French doctor, having discovered my plight, moved heaven and earth with the authorities to get me released. In the end, I was freed, on parole, with my doctor friend made fully responsible for my person and conduct. Now, as regards Dr Garnier, I stand in the shoes of my old friend in Normandy. I am responsible for his safety and conduct here. You understand?'

'Yes, Miss Redpath, I do. But, until Superintendent Littlejohn arrives from France and we are able to consult him and decide on the next step, I shall have to leave a constable here to keep Dr Garnier under surveillance. Not only that, but it is obvious that the doctor has an enemy who is anxious to dispose of him. I am, therefore, concerned for his safety.'

The doctor laughed.

'You mean Grimaud?'

'Yes. He seems to be the villain of the piece. What had he against you?'

'That is a long tale, Inspector, and I hope you'll have patience to bear with me and let me rest a little before I begin it.'

'Of course, doctor. But tell me one thing. I've only just left hospital after recovering from a blow on the head which rendered me thoroughly unconscious. Judging from the circumstances, you were responsible for the attack. Am I right?'

'No, you are not. I was either unconscious or tied-up myself when you arrived. I was being prepared for my journey across to Ireland which ended more fortunately for me than was intended.'

'So it was Springer?'

'Presumably. From all accounts, I should now be dead. Since my arrival here, I have been twice beaten-up, blown-up in a boat, set on fire, and forced to swim between seven and ten miles in a semi-conscious condition. The human body can tolerate and recover from very much abuse and I, as a surgeon, have seen many examples of it. But quite seriously, I think I now hold the record. We are up against a very desperate and resourceful antagonist. I know that from the past. But he is growing old, like the rest of us, and losing his ruthless enterprise. That will soon be his undoing.'

17

LAST SPIN OF THE WHEEL

I t was evening when Littlejohn and his party arrived back in the Isle of Man and they were met by Knell at the airport. Thence, to Grenaby.

Much to the annoyance of Maggie Keggin, who had prepared a special spread by way of a welcome home, Knell, urged mainly by the Archdeacon, gave them a full report of developments since they had left the Island. It was after seven before the meal ended and by that time the party had decided on a plan of campaign. Speed was essential, as Springer was still at large, albeit Orrisdale Hall was under close surveillance by the local police.

'A man of his type, trained as a commando during the war, and chosen to be dropped in France to guard an important scientist, could very easily give the best of policemen the slip if he were alarmed and decided to take flight,' said Dorange. 'So far, if what your men say is true, he is still at home, carrying on his customary ways. He must still think his plan to dispose of Dr Garnier has succeeded and that he is free from any suspicion. Once he becomes aware that Garnier is alive and on the Island, he will become desperate. It is time the case was wound up and finished with.'

It was decided that it would be unwise for all four of them to erupt on Dr Garnier at Fleshwick and Littlejohn and Knell made the journey together to give the Superintendent a first-hand story of Allasac's adventures. Dorange remained with the Archdeacon at Grenaby.

They had landed on the Island in the dusk of a splendid summer day. It was warm and sunny and the first sight from the air of the magnificent coastline and the gentle contours behind it was spectacular. Dorange, who, in spite of the enthusiastic accounts of the place from Littlejohn and the Archdeacon, had thought of it as a sort of glorified Coney Island, was speechless. Which amused Littlejohn, who had never found the famous Frenchman short of a word before.

Now, he seemed quite happy to take his ease in the twilight with the Archdeacon and Mrs Littlejohn and was content to leave Knell and Littlejohn with the case.

They came upon Dr Garnier and Miss Redpath playing cards with Quinney, their official custodian. Quinney would have found sitting or parading around very tedious had not the doctor suggested they might play some game or other. Quinney was just learning to play chess, but as there were no chessmen available they had descended to cards and he had been teaching the doctor and Miss Redpath solo whist. Garnier had insisted on stakes to add interest and Quinney now found himself embarrassed by the pile of coppers at his elbow when Knell arrived.

'Opened another casino, Quinney?' said Knell as Quinney, abetted by Miss Redpath, awkwardly pocketed his winnings and then stood to attention.

Knell introduced Littlejohn, Miss Redpath served coffee and they asked the doctor to repeat the account of his adventures, recently told to Knell, for Littlejohn's benefit.

'I have just left your brother and sister in Evian and they were delighted to hear that you are safe and well, doctor. They have been a great help to us in our investigations.'

'I'm afraid, Superintendent, they only know half the story. Aimée is a very talkative woman and one has to be careful what one confides in her. Frédéric, on the other hand, though a very sympathetic man and a brilliant lawyer, is restricted by the rules of his profession. He must work within the law and I fear the affair in which poor Sylvie and I were engaged was hardly legal. To have confided in Frédéric that we were on our way to kill a man would have placed him in a very embarrassing position. However, now that the case is in the hands of the police, I am content to tell you all I know and what has happened.'

'Please begin with the death of your brother on the night he attempted to escape to Lausanne.'

'It goes farther back than that. Back to the days in the Grande Chartreuse. I take it you already know the general outline of what happened there.'

'Yes. The police at Thonon were very well informed about it and Father Laurent, of the Grande Chartreuse monastery, filled in some of the details...'

'You met Father Laurent? A fine man. He is well?'

'Very well, I gather. My friends Dorange, of the Nice Sûreté, and the Archdeacon of Man, who accompanied me to Evian, interviewed him. He was allowed to speak with them and was a great help.'

'Good! Well... Let us begin with the arrival of Alice Faure at the Grande Chartreuse. She came to us from the Vercors group, part of which had been betrayed and had found it necessary to transfer elsewhere. She arrived with papers quite in order, recommended and vouched for by undoubted people and, as she was a trained nurse, a good shot, and an enthusiastic patriot — or so we thought — we were glad to welcome her. We had no idea that she was a clever Vichy spy and in touch with the Gestapo. Her arrival coincided with the making of plans for harassing the enemy during the imminent invasion of allied troops in southern Europe. The man we knew as Grimaud, my brother Edouard's

177

bodyguard, seems to have taken a fancy to Alice from the start. Before long, it was suspected than an affair was going on between them…'

Garnier, whose wounds seemed to be growing uncomfortable, moved here and there on the couch until he was settled again.

'That's better. She was a good-looking, interesting woman and isolated from the world, almost imprisoned together between sorties… well… such things happened. It did not greatly worry us, until my brother became involved. Suddenly, he developed not a fancy, but a passion for Alice Faure and she seemed to feel the same about him. That was serious, for Edouard's wife was with him. Also, rivalry between two men for a woman, when one of the men is the bodyguard of the other, is, to say the least of it, embarrassing. When I visited the group in the course of my rounds of medical duties, the leader, a professor from Grenoble, known as Perrache, asked me to speak with my brother about it, as all his own talks with Edouard had been fruitless. He said he was arranging for Alice Faure to leave for another distant group in the near future. You see, at that time, a large attack on a railway near Grenoble was being planned, they needed every available member of the group and, until it was completed, Alice would have to remain. The plan was put into operation, it failed, probably because it was betrayed by Alice Faure, and all those involved were killed except my brother Edouard and Grimaud who managed to get away to my mother's place at Evian.'

Dr Garnier spoke slowly, choosing his words carefully. Quite a different man from the impression Littlejohn had gathered of him in Evian, where he seemed to take second place to his more flamboyant brother, Frédéric. He was now quite self-possessed and in control of the situation.

'They only stayed at Evian one night, for the Vichy police were on their heels. Their only way of escape was across the lake to neutral territory in Switzerland and they planned to cross to Lausanne by night. I was detained in Grenoble at the time, but my sister-in-law, Sylvie, told me what happened. I suppose you know Edouard was killed; Grimaud got away.'

'You learned the results of the enquiry into your brother's death, doctor?'

'Yes. We had our contacts among loyal friends. He died of a bullet from a small calibre gun, which seemed to rule out the fact that Grimaud had shot him rather than let him be captured by the Germans. I should tell you, that that was one of the orders given to Grimaud before he left London for France. Fearful that Edouard and his atomic knowledge might at any time fall in enemy hands, Grimaud had orders to shoot him rather than allow him to be captured. Who could have fired the small bullet then? Grimaud, an army officer, regularly carried a large Smith and Wesson. All of us, his comrades, knew it well and admired it. It would, fired from the distance from which Edouard was reported to have been shot, have blown his head off.'

He paused to light a cigarette and then resumed.

'Instead, he met his death from a gun which was comparatively a toy, which could almost be carried in the vest pocket. Now came a strange thing. The autopsy, the results of which were not, of course, made public in the circumstances for the Vichy police wished it to be thought that *they* had killed my brother, the autopsy revealed that the bullet was fired from a gun of the type which my brother himself carried. My sister-in-law, his wife, who knew of his affair with the Faure woman and suffered a serious nervous collapse as a result, accompanied him and Grimaud part of the way to the spot where their boat was to meet them. She told me that my brother was then carrying his small Beretta pistol. All in all, it appeared that he might have shot himself rather than be arrested by his pursuers.'

He paused and took a drink of his cold coffee.

'But an event a few days afterwards convinced us that this was not the case. A Resistance agent informed us that Alice Faure had been found shot in her flat in Lausanne by a bullet from a gun similar to the one which had killed Edouard. The inference was obvious. By some trick or perhaps by force, Grimaud had obtained my brother's gun from him, shot him — presumably to rid himself of his rival for Alice Faure's affections — and then, for some reason — it may have been in a quarrel — killed Alice when he met her in Lausanne.'

Littlejohn thrust his hand in his pocket and produced the gun found in Madame Sylvie Garnier's handbag.

'Is that the gun you are speaking of?'

Dr Garnier leaned over and took up the weapon.

'Where did you come by this?'

'It is the gun which killed your sister-in-law in Douglas and was later found in her handbag hidden in some bushes on the promenade.'

'But this has not been in circulation since Sylvie saw it in her husband's possession on the night he was shot.'

'Except in the hands of her murderer, whose name is now obvious. Grimaud, or Springer, took it with him after killing your brother and Alice Faure and used it to kill your sister-in-law. Are you sure this is the right gun?'

'I'm quite sure. It was mine. I bought it before the war when my practice took me in some strange places. I never used it. I gave it to Edouard when he left to join the Resistance. He was never a violent man and had none of his own. Yes, this is the gun. Is it loaded?'

'Partially. Four shots have been fired from the magazine. One killed Madame Garnier and one was used by the Manx police to establish the fact. The others were fired by the French ballistic authorities, who, with the help of their Swiss colleagues, identified the bullets which killed your brother and Alice Faure.'

Garnier handed it back to Littlejohn, who passed it to Knell.

'You'd better take charge of that, Knell. It's really the property of the Manx police now.'

And Knell thrust it in his own pocket without a word.

'Have you the record you obtained from London, Knell?'

During Littlejohn's absence, Knell had been checking the career of Colonel Springer. He now produced the papers from his pocket and handed them over. Littlejohn passed them to Dr Garnier.

'I wish I'd had this years ago, Littlejohn. Sylvie and I, after we learned of Edouard's death and the manner of it, were anxious to meet Grimaud. As I will tell you later, we actually did, but twenty years after Edouard's death, and we came very badly out of it, as you know. I fully intended that if I ever caught up with him, and he could not give me a satisfactory account, I would shoot him in cold blood. It was the only way to obtain justice. You see so many crimes of this kind, so many settlings of old scores, were committed under cover of the Resistance and, as often as not, have never been solved and even if they were solved, were frequently overlooked under amnesty arrangements. No. If we required justice, we would have to act on our own initiative.'

He cast his eyes over the paper in his hand.

'I see that Springer is not his real name. He changed it from Walker when he left the army. It seems that after the murder, Grimaud escaped and arrived in London. Quite a number of internees escaped from Switzerland. Then, perhaps afraid that his crimes might come home to roost and he might suffer the consequences, he deserted and went abroad. Kenya, it is thought. He was, it says, not a professional soldier, but a wine salesman before the war. Now, it would seem, he has returned to the British Isles and to the quiet Isle of Man, where a man might safely hide from his pursuers for ever. Who would suspect that he'd hidden here? And then, by a curious turn of fate, a casino is established, Sylvie arrives to try her hand, and of all things, finds Grimaud playing roulette one night. He had grown too confident and was showing himself in public, sure, no doubt, that none of his old associates in the Resistance would ever find their way here.'

He handed the record back to Knell and thanked him.

'And your sister-in-law sent for you?'

Dr Garnier nodded.

'Yes. She sent for me. I was very anxious about her. She was alone and unarmed. My brother, Frédéric, lent his revolver to her, as she often had large sums in her possession from her roulette winnings. She laughed at the idea, at the time. She accepted it, as she did not wish to offend him, but handed it to me for safe-keeping. Now, Springer has that too. He took it from me the first time we met. A very formidable man, Springer.'

'You came here at once. What then?'

'I arrived about 5.30 in the evening. I telephoned Sylvie from the airport at the number she had given me. She told me she had seen Grimaud at the casino and had found on enquiry there that he was resident on the Island, was an enthusiastic gambler and frequently played there. She said she proposed facing him next time she saw him. She asked me to meet her in the casino forecourt that night at eleven o'clock. The reason for the late appointment was that she didn't wish Grimaud to see me about the town, take alarm, and flee. She told me I had not changed much since Grimaud knew me; she, on the other hand *had* changed, she said, and until she faced him and revealed her identity, she was sure he wouldn't recognise her. Grimaud must have arrived unexpectedly at the casino, seen and recognised her, unknown to Sylvie, and when she took her nightly walk before I arrived, he followed and shot her. He must have thought she had traced his whereabouts and was searching for him in the Isle of Man. His conscience must still have been troubling him and he could not risk her finding him and stirring up trouble about his crimes of years ago.'

Littlejohn nodded.

'That must be the reason for his searching her room after her death. He had to know that nothing connected with Madame Garnier pointed in his direction. He took her keys from her bag and, to rid himself of the gun, put it in the bag which he hid under a bush in the promenade gardens.

'Then, he searched her room, presumably to check her identity and make sure that nothing in her possessions, written or otherwise, might incriminate him. He missed the false bottom in her suitcase and all the money it contained. But what of your side of the case, sir?'

Dr Garnier was looking thoroughly jaded, but in spite of the protests of Miss Redpath, insisted on finishing his account. More coffee arrived and, to give Garnier a breathing space, Littlejohn told Quinney, who had been sitting in one corner, almost asleep from the heat of the room, to find the nearest phone-box, ring Grenaby Parsonage and let the Archdeacon and Dorange know that he proposed to visit Orrisdale Hall that night and that he would pick them up on his way.

Then Garnier went on with his story.

'I kept my appointment in the forecourt of the casino at eleven o'clock, but Sylvie did not appear. Just after eleven I heard a passer-by telling another that an old lady had been found murdered on the beach. I knew it was Sylvie...'

'And then?'

'I knew who had done it. I was angry and almost out of my mind with grief and chagrin. I went inside the hotel to get a drink and book a room for the night. And there, descending the staircase, I encountered Grimaud face to face.'

'He must have been returning from searching Madame Garnier's room.'

'I did a very foolish thing. Instead of passing him by without apparently recognising him, I quietly accosted him and surprised him. He *was* surprised, believe me. He looked as if he'd seen a ghost. He must have thought Sylvie was alone. As for me, I'd a lot of questions to ask Grimaud before I thought of going to the police or killing him myself. He soon recovered his aplomb. He asked if I were alone and I said I was. I didn't even mention Sylvie's death and he daren't speak of her. Each of us knew the other was challenging him, but no word was spoken of it. A grim game seemed to be beginning and it was played-out to my disadvantage and discomfiture. I casually said I had just been booking a room in the hotel. He then actually invited me to stay with him whilst I was in the Isle of Man. I knew he intended to dispose of me as he had done my sister-in-law, but he wanted time to think out a plan and gather his thoughts about it. Nevertheless, I accepted.'

Dr Garnier took a good drink of coffee.

'There's not much more. Grimaud had his car in the park nearby. We went for it and then occurred a long drive through the dark. Through the town and then into the country, with the lights of villages as we passed through. That part of the road was excellent. We almost felt to be flying, instead of driving in a fast car. Then, we turned suddenly along a road which was overhung with trees and I could hear a river running somewhere. Up a steep hill and finally we seemed to reach the wilderness. A long road on a sort of plateau... We spoke little on the way. It was as though each of us was expecting something and planning how to meet it...'

Garnier, living through it again, was perspiring heavily. He mopped his forehead.

'May I have a little brandy and soda, please, my dear?'

Miss Redpath returned with glasses and a syphon and served drinks all round. She protested to Garnier again that he was doing himself harm, but he was determined to finish.

'I am not an impulsive man, but I hate suspense. Under the strain of it, I usually grasp the nettle and be done with it. I did that in the middle of our wild ride. I determined to challenge Grimaud forthwith. I took out Frédéric's revolver, which I had brought with me, and told him to stop, as I had something I wished to discuss with him and some questions to ask. I thrust the gun in his back and made him climb out of the car, as I thought he might play some trick on me and wished to see his every move.'

Garnier smiled and shrugged his shoulders.

'I would make a very poor tactician in battle. I had placed

Grimaud in a position of advantage by making him face me. I had also forgotten that during the war he had the training of a commando and was an adept in unarmed combat. Before I knew what had happened, he had struck me a smashing blow over the heart, felled me in the road, and seized the gun. We fought in the light of the car headlamps. I don't recollect the details. I knew that if I allowed him any chances, he would kill me. I scrambled to my feet, but he did not fire. Instead, he aimed a furious kick at my head. In the uncertain light, he must have misjudged it, for I caught his leg as it descended, gripped it, rolled on my side, and heaved him in the hedge. I remember, funnily enough, two cars passed us as we struggled. Neither stopped. They must have been eager to get home or else unwilling to be mixed-up in our affairs... In the respite whilst Grimaud struggled in the hedge, I took to my heels and ran. There was a cottage nearby, with a lighted bedroom window. I hardly knew what I was doing after the beating-up I'd received, but I made for the house and I just hadn't the energy to open the gate of the garden and knock on the door. I hung over the gate, exhausted, shouting for help. Luckily a woman was awake in the upper-room, took me in before Grimaud caught up with me, and was a great help.'

'That was Mrs Craine. She told us about it.'

'Indeed! So you traced me there. I must call to thank her for her great service as soon as I am mobile again. I'm afraid I did a very discourteous thing. As soon as she left me to myself, I sneaked out into the night. You see, I thought Grimaud would follow me there. I felt physically helpless to resist. So I fled again. Grimaud was waiting for me not more than a hundred yards away. I didn't even see him. He hit me over the head, probably with my own gun. And that is all I clearly remember until I found myself securely trussed-up in a room in what must have been Grimaud's house. It was then daylight, presumably early morning. I remained there in that condition for what seemed about two days and nights. Grimaud gave me some food, then tied me up again. I could hear dogs barking and cocks crowing, but little else. And, during that time, he had callers once. I heard their voices, but was gagged and could not make myself heard. He must have been waiting for something. I didn't know what...'

'Waiting for a chance to get you down to a quiet spot on the coast and put you in his boat, I guess.'

'That would be it. I don't know why he didn't shoot me out of hand.'

'In case any of the trails led to him, he didn't want to be landed with a body, which, wherever he hid it, might come to light. His worry was that he didn't know what Madame Garnier had said to anyone, maybe the police, during her stay in the Isle of Man. The callers you mentioned were the police from Peel. Another visitor, Inspector Knell, was promptly hit over the head and rendered unconscious. Your presence there indicated that Madame Garnier had some plan in mind. Grimaud didn't know what she planned and used the utmost caution. An accident, such as he was contriving for you, would, at least free him from guilt and suspicion in your case.'

'I suppose so. It seems to have been misplaced caution. That was one of his irritating characteristics when he was with us in the Resistance. However, that was the state of things until he entered the room in which I was lying on a bed and with cold-blooded deliberation, hit me over the head and rendered me unconscious again. That is all I remember until I became dimly aware that I was at sea and in grave danger.'

'Grimaud, alias Springer, had concocted a very plausible tale indeed about you, doctor, firmly fixing the murder of Madame Garnier on your shoulders. Like the rest of us at the time, he naturally could not invent a motive, but he showed great skill in placing the guilt on you. He even trussed himself up very tightly under the stairs and said you had done it in order to get away with his car and his boat. He also told us about the days when you and he were in the Resistance in France. In fact, a complete and ingenious story of your perfidy from beginning to end. He must have known that Mrs Craine gave you hospitality and would report it to the police and they would start investigating the affair. He couldn't kill Mrs Craine to silence her. He therefore had to find a good story to cover your appearance and disappearance.'

'Most ingenious.'

'Yes. Except that two little flaws sowed the seeds of doubt in our minds. The first was the matter of his dogs. He has two rather formidable sporting dogs loose on the premises. When Inspector Knell first visited the hall, he saw nobody around and before he could thoroughly investigate matters, he was knocked unconscious. Later, Grimaud or Springer, was found tied-up under the stairs. Knell must have arrived just as Springer was preparing you for your sea trip. He knocked Knell out. Then, later, seeing other police on the way, trussed himself up under the stairs. He told the story that it was all your work. Knell said that when he arrived, he thought he heard the whimpering of dogs. But not the barking. Now that pair of dogs would have barked their heads off at such an intrusion had not Springer been there and free to keep them quiet. *You* wouldn't have been able to do it. It led us to think there was something fishy about Springer's story. The other strange thing which made us suspicious was that your so-called heart-attack seemed more like the results of a good beating-up than anything else. When you and Springer were found to be involved, it seemed to us that Springer might have been the cause of the injuries. We never trusted him. Too glib and too cocksure.'

'A most interesting affair. My "murder", planned by Grimaud, was most ingenious and drawn on what one might term massive lines on a huge canvas. Wasn't it?'

'It was indeed. And now, we must be off to visit Mr Grimaud. We'll see what he has to say for himself. Meanwhile, however, a man will be sent to relieve P.C. Quinney. We must take no risks.'

'I am still under suspicion, then?'

'No, doctor. But until the case is cleared, we have certain duties...'

It was past eleven when Littlejohn, Dorange and Knell arrived at Orrisdale Hall. The Archdeacon, tired after a long day's travel, had been persuaded by his visitors and ordered by Maggie Keggin to retire to bed.

There was a light in the living-room downstairs when they approached the place. The dogs were already barking savagely as they parked the car by the door of the courtyard. The three men made their way to the front door by the path round the house. As they passed the lighted window, the curtains of which were still drawn back, they could see the table set for a meal with a book propped against a jampot as though the occupant had been disturbed by the dogs as he was eating. Springer was standing near the door of the room, with his head cocked, listening.

Knell knocked on the front door and Springer quickly appeared. He strained to make them out and then recoiled a bit.

'Police? What do you want at this time? Have you made an arrest in the murder case?'

'No. But we'd like to ask you one or two questions.'

'You'd better come in, although I must say... I was just getting ready for bed.'

Dorange in the gloom spoke to Littlejohn in French.

Littlejohn didn't reply, but explained to Springer.

'This is Mr Dorange, a friend of the Archdeacon of Man. with whom I'm staying. He has driven us here, although he won't come in. Matters we wish to discuss are official. He'll wait in the car.'

Springer looked closely at Dorange in the darkness and then spoke to him in French. They exchanged a word or two, trivialities. Dorange congratulated Springer on his excellent French. He told Dorange he had spent quite a time in France during the war. And that before the war, as a wine merchant, he'd lived for two years near Beaune and learned the language thoroughly.

Dorange thanked him and said he'd now leave them and wait in the car.

Springer persisted in speaking French.

'Don't stay out in the dark. Come in with your friends and have a drink.'

But Dorange insisted that police work was of no interest to him. He was a carnation grower from Nice, he said. And with that he ended the argument by leaving them. He was anxious to act as a second line of defence in case anything went wrong. From all accounts, Springer was a desperate and enterprising character.

Inside, a log fire was burning in the hearth and the dogs, still uneasy, were sitting on the rug attentively. Springer dismissed them peremptorily and they retired to a corner.

'Drink? It's a bit chilly.'

'No, thanks. We're anxious to get back. It's a bit late.'

'You're telling me. Couldn't this have waited till tomorrow?'

'Having come all this way, sir, we'd better finish it.'

Without more ado, Littlejohn asked Knell for the gun and placed it on the table.

'Have you ever seen this before, Colonel Springer?'

Springer hesitated and covered his momentary discomfiture by taking up the weapon and examining it. He placed it back on the table.

'No. Never seen it before. Why?'

'It looks a harmless little thing, but it has already killed three people.'

'What has that to do with me?'

'Edouard Garnier, Alice Faure and Madame Sylvie Garnier, all well known to you, sir.'

'What of it? It's not mine.'

'But has been in your possession for more than twenty years.'

'Rubbish. Who told you that?'

'It was originally the property of Allasac, Dr Ambroise Garnier, who was blown-up recently in your boat.'

'What's all the fuss about, then? Why bring me in this? He killed Madame Garnier, presumably for the money she'd won at roulette and then met a suitable end. Am I supposed to identify the weapon? Because if I am, you're barking up the wrong tree.'

'Dr Garnier was blown-up but survived…'

'What! You've got him then? Jolly good!'

'I'm surprised you say that after all the trouble you took to kill him!'

'Look here…'

'First you tied him up whilst you went by night to bring your boat from Peel to the shore near here. Then to make it appear that Allasac had stolen your boat from Peel harbour, you'd to make it seem that he also took your car to get to Peel. Did you walk home after you left your car in the park on the quay? You must have had a job handling a heavy man like Allasac.'

'What the hell are you raving about? Not a word of it is true.'

'Over the past few days, we've been accumulating some interesting past history about the Grenoble Resistance in the Grande Chartreuse and the end of Professor Edouard Garnier. Your mistress, Alice Faure, is thought to have betrayed a Resistance plan to blow up a section of railway line with the result that all the Resistance men concerned were killed, except you and Edouard Garnier. The two of you fled to Evian where, in attempting to escape by boat to Switzerland, Garnier was killed. Not by the Vichy police or military, but by a bullet from his own gun. The gun you have just handled. You alone escaped. A few days later, the gun was used to kill Alice Faure in Lausanne. How did it get across to Lausanne, sir? You were the only one who crossed. Add to this the fact that before you and Garnier attempted the crossing the Vichy police were warned of the matter by a voice over the telephone. A disguised voice. But whoever did it couldn't hide one peculiarity. He rolled his Rs like a true Burgundian. You learned French in Burgundy, colonel, didn't you? And you still roll you Rs in the local fashion. My friend Dorange, who speaks good English, as well, confirmed that just now.'

'You are a clever lot, aren't you? And where do I come in? There are thousands who roll their Rs in France. It doesn't apply only to Burgundians. And now, if you've finished, I'll bid you good night and get to bed.'

'Not tonight, sir. We have proof that the gun which killed Madame Garnier has been in your possession for more than twenty years. Ever since you killed Alice Faure. We have also many of your contemporaries in the French Resistance lined-up with evidence about almost every step you made until you killed Alice Faure. And now, I must ask you to accompany us to Douglas police station, where you will be questioned further, after being charged with the murder of Madame Sylvie Garnier. You need say nothing more, but I must tell you that anything you say may be used in evidence...'

Springer said nothing. Instead, he moved to one corner where two sporting guns were resting, seized one, and levelled it at Littlejohn.

'That will be enough. Your deductions and enquiries are a pack of nonsense and I'm not returning to Douglas or any other police station...'

'Put that down, Springer...'

'Not on your life. And if either of you moves a step nearer, I'll let you have it and blow you to kingdom come.'

He moved slowly towards the desk in the corner, opened a drawer with one hand and drew out a large Smith and Wesson revolver.

'That's better. This is loaded; the gun wasn't. I'm more at home with my pistol. Now...'

He looked pleased with himself.

'Now. I've gone so far. No reason why I shouldn't go the whole hog and give the police a killing worthwhile. I ought to shoot the lot of you. But I'm going to grant you a sporting chance. I'm going to give you a spell in gaol yourselves. A taste of your own medicine. That will give me just the flying start I need.'

'By sea, I suppose, only this time, the boat won't blow up...'

'That's my affair. Call in your friend. And no funny stuff. I'd a thorough training in all the tricks and one false move and the shooting will start. Call him... Open the window there and shout that all's well and I'm going with you to Douglas. Just that; no more. But come here first. Both of you turn your backs to me.'

With quick skill he ran his hands over their pockets, turning out the gun from Knell's possession.

'Now, your friend.'

Littlejohn called Dorange who meekly entered and allowed himself to be frisked as well.

'Now, stand with your backs to me and your hands behind you.'

They obeyed like an obedient squad of new recruits.

'Across the yard I've a nice little private prison. The last tenant of this place kept pigs in it. It was built by the original owner more than a century ago. He had a brother who was a raving madman and had to be kept under restraint. Those were his quarters. A solid door and a window a bit larger than a postage stamp. You're all going to take a little holiday there until the postman arrives tomorrow afternoon. That is, if he has any mail for me, which is unlikely. I don't get many letters. In that case you'll have to wait three days for the grocer's van. I've two loaves and I'll give you a can of water. You can consider yourselves very lucky. I could just as easily shoot you all in the back. And now, we'll march and inspect our billets and I'll see you safely tucked in. Hands above heads, now.'

They all obeyed. Springer seemed to be enjoying himself.

'Single file, quick march. And any tricks and I'll shoot the one nearest me the first. I'm sorry we can't all have a little talk and compare notes, but I must be getting on my way.'

He took up a large electric lamp, switched it on, and they

marched out and through the front door like a floodlit awkward squad.

Dorange brought up the rear, followed cautiously by Springer who kept a safe distance behind. He seemed to have sensed that Dorange was from the French police and knew that they were as handy with their feet as with their fists.

'Straight ahead and across the yard to the corner...'

Past the illuminated living-room window and then the kitchen, now in darkness. As the flood of light from the living-room changed to the gloom illuminated only by Springer's lamp, Dorange suddenly acted. His left arm flashed downwards in an arc and swept from the outside kitchen window-sill the gun he had left there when he entered the house. As soon as he touched the gun, it seemed to go off, Springer growled and both the lamp and his revolver clattered to the ground. The bullet had caught him in the shoulder. Before the three men could pounce on him, Springer had fallen on his gun. There was a second shot.

'Save you the trouble,' he said, and died.

'I'd been watching the little pantomime through the window all the time,' Dorange told them afterwards. 'When you called me, Tom, I left my spare gun outside in the dark and tucked the small one in the top of my sock. I always carry two. Sooner or later, I managed to get my hand on one of them...'

They had to raid the stock of brandy in Springer's sideboard to restore their morale before they left. When Springer's belongings at Orrisdale Hall were gone through, there was found, among other interesting things, a photograph of Alice Faure, identical with that in Edouard Garnier's cigarette case. It was signed *Toujours, Alice.*

Dr Ambroise Garnier, after a complete recovery, married Grace Redpath at Grenaby church and the Archdeacon officiated. Meanwhile, the same team that had solved the mystery of Madame Garnier's death set cheerfully to work on another task, that of finishing the erection of the Archdeacon's new conservatory. This was done in record time and when Dorange returned home, he sent a parcel of his father's famous carnation plants to grace it. And, as the customs officers are always eager to pounce upon and impound such imports, their arrival at Grenaby was still another mystery.

INTRUDER IN THE DARK

GEORGE BELLAIRS

1

THE DISGRUNTLED LEGATEE

The small family car descended with brake-lights flashing on and off as Mr. Cyril Savage checked his downhill flight. A corner, a little planation of old birch trees and then the village of Plumpton Bois strewn along each side of the main road and creeping into the hillsides behind it.

'Here we are,' he said to his wife.

The car stopped with a shudder and they both craned their necks to see what it was like.

It was early afternoon and there didn't seem anybody about. In front of the village pub, a large black dog was asleep with its muzzle between its outstretched forepaws. On a seat by the door, an old man was snoozing, his chin on his hands supported by the handle of a walking-stick wedged between his knees. Farther down the road, two parked old cars and an unattended lorry loaded with sacks of coal.

The inn itself was a small primitive affair with a faded sign over the door. *Miners Arms*. A name quite out of place nowadays, though not so a century ago. Plumpton Bois had then been a busy community where fortunes were being made in mining a lot of lead and a little silver. Then the lodes had run out and so had the miners and the mining companies. Rows of empty cottages had stood derelict and the larger houses of the officials had been the same. The place became a deserted village occupied only by a sprinkling of those whose roots seemed to have sunk too deeply to be moved.

Then, during the war, the great heaps of slag and rubbish and the stones and the rusty iron of the engine-houses, offices and weigh-houses of the deserted mines had been carted away for road-making and defence works, the wreckage had been covered by nature with a carpet of grass and wild flowers and somebody, finding beauty at last in the setting among the hills, had bought a decent house there for an old song and renovated it. In less than two years the village was almost fully occupied again, this time by week-end and summer retreats of the inhabitants of nearby towns. It even attracted some commuters.

Nevertheless, it was a deserted place for much of its existence. The owners of the small houses once alive with the lusty families of the miners, now only visited them in their leisure. For the rest of the time, most of them were shut up and locked, their modern shutters closed and their gaily painted doors fastened and staring blindly on the village street.

Mr. Savage entered the inn. It smelled of alcohol and garlic. The interior somewhat belied the drab outside. Mr. Crabb, the landlord, who met the intruder in his shirt sleeves, had been slowly adapting himself to the influx of new blood and ideas in the village. There was a project in embryo for tearing down the *Miners Arms* and rebuilding it, with a swimming pool behind and a new name to match. *Plumpton Bois Auberge.* People liked that kind of thing after holidays on the Continent. They also liked foreign cooking which accounted for the prevailing aroma of garlic. Mrs. Crabb had started making meals in the evenings; French cuisine gathered from recipes in ladies' magazines.

Mr. Crabb showed no enthusiasm when he saw his visitor at that time in the afternoon. Furthermore, Savage exhibited no signs of thirst or wishing to drink. In fact, he had the look of a teetotaller. He had on his face the enquiring expression of a lost traveller.

'Could you tell me where I can find a house called *Johnsons Place?*'

'I'll show you ...'

Mr. Crabb sought a cap from under the bar. He had a bald head and quickly took cold, although he persisted in his shirt sleeves.

He put on the cap and shuffled to the front door — for he was still wearing his carpet slippers — gently towing Mr. Savage along with him. They faced the view across the valley. Not a soul in sight; not a breath of wind. On that sunny day it was magnificent. A green hillside sparsely dotted with old trees and divided into small square fields with cattle feeding in them or else crops flourishing there. A stream ran in the valley between the inn and the hills.

Mr. Crabb pointed downstream to where in a patch of greenery a stone bridge crossed the water.

'See the bridge? Cross it. It's the first house on the left. A biggish, stone place in a fair sized garden. Used to belong to a Miss Melody Johnson who died about a month ago. Very old lady. Past eighty.'

'Yes I know. She was my great-aunt.'

'Oh, was she? Fancy that. Didn't know she had any relations. None came during her last illness.'

'I didn't even know she was ill. In fact, I only knew she was dead when the lawyer wrote.'

Mr. Crabb gave him a reproachful look, as though, somehow, he thought Mr. Savage had been neglecting his duty.

'I have inherited *Johnsons Place* under my great-aunt's will. I'm on my way with my wife to see it now for the first time. This seems a nice locality.'

'Not bad. Not bad. Live near here?'

'No. Our home is in London. We started out early this morning and hope to be back again there late tonight. We're just here to look over the place and then we'll decide what to do about it.'

'Thinking of selling? Because it should go for quite a nice figure. Since they did-up this village the value of property has gone up quite a lot. There's been a lot of enquiries about *Johnsons Place* already. It's commodious and in a lovely position.'

Savage made no answer, but moved towards the car where his wife sat watching his every move and even seemed to be trying to read his lips and fathom what he and the landlord were talking about.

'Well, thank you, landlord.'

Mr. Crabb shuffled off and left the pair together again. They followed his instructions, downhill and across the bridge which carried a byway into the hills beyond. They quickly found the house.

The garden stood neglected and overgrown and as Savage gazed at it, it seemed to grow more vast and forbidding. He felt a mood of melancholy and frustration seize him. He had played with the idea of taking over the place himself if it suited him and his wife. The thought of setting to rights this wilderness filled him with despair. He was a tall, spare, middle-aged man with a long, serious face, quite devoid of humour. His looks now grew harassed and petulant at his thoughts. He turned to his wife and shrugged. Her expression was almost exactly like his own, except that she was nearer to tears.

'Oh, dear!'

It was very hot and still and the surrounding trees and over-grown hedges oppressed the visitors almost to suffocation. The neighbourhood seemed deserted. A few birds twittered in the bushes and in the distance someone was rushing hither and thither on a tractor.

All the blinds of the house were drawn. It stood back from the gate at the end of the worn-out path and its soiled white façade was sad-looking and desolate. An oblong structure, low lying and sprawling, with a door in the middle of the front with a window on each side of it. Three windows upstairs and a kind of glazed trap-door in the roof. A large stone doorstep, hollowed out in the middle by the feet of long-forgotten people. There was a neglected hen-run — a wire-netting enclosure with a tumble-down shed in one corner — at one end, apparently left just as it was after the poultry had been disposed of. As Savage approached, a rat ran from the shed and disappeared in the hedge.

The two intruders made their way slowly along the path. Now and then they stumbled over protruding cobblestones which bristled underfoot.

Savage paused before they reached the door. He was obviously displeased. He was disappointed with everything: the village itself, the house, the damp abandon, the smell and decay, the solitude … the lot.

He did not complain to his wife. There seemed too much to grumble about. He was hostile to the whole set-up and was now growing hostile to his wife, as well, for suggesting the visit there, although it was necessary and had to be made sometime or other. He trudged slowly to the door and took out the key which the lawyer had given him. Then, he paused and looked back as though someone other than his companion were following him.

There was a view of the village between the trees. The scattered houses irregularly lining each side of the main road. The church tower with its rusty weathercock protruding through a thick mass of leaves. The abandoned Methodist chapel — 'Erected to the Glory of God 1852' — near the by-road to *Johnsons Place*. To Mr. Savage it was all depressing. He contemplated it with a strange dread, like a man condemned to exile from a beloved place inspecting his future prison.

There was a bell-push on the door jamb and for something better to do as her husband hesitated, Mrs. Savage gently tugged it. There was a creak of old wire and somewhere, far away, a ghostly bell pealed in the darkness of the house.

Mr. Savage jumped.

'What are you doing?' he said hoarsely as though his wife were tinkering with something dangerous.

He inserted the key in the lock and opened the door, which resisted him at first. Then a fetid draught of air surrounded the pair on the threshold. It reeked of damp stone floors, stored rotten apples and the greasy stench of neglected kitchens.

They entered hesitantly, as though afraid to disturb some waiting occupant, and found themselves plunged in cold and darkness. Mr. Savage almost ran to the window at the end of the passage and with difficulty drew up the yellow blind. A thin trickle of light spread down the long, narrow corridor from the soiled window, half obscured by an overgrowth of dead old roses and leaves from the bushes outside.

They could make out two doors to rooms on the left and right of the passage and another one to the kitchens to the right beyond. The passage was floored in old-fashioned red and cream tiles and furnished with a hat stand of bamboo, two chairs, pictures on the walls, a coconut mat on the floor. To the left at the far end, the stairs ascended.

Mr. Savage's aunt had left him the house as it stood, furniture and all, and he was anxious to inspect his windfall. He didn't quite know what to expect among the goods and chattels of the dead woman. He had never been here before. Admitted, Miss Melody Johnson had been his great-aunt. But she might just as well have been a stranger. She had been his grandfather's sister and both of them had been born at *Johnsons Place* along with two other sisters and another brother, all of whom had died before his grandfather. Grandfather Johnson had left home early in life. He had never taken to mining or the life in Plumpton Bois, had quarrelled with his father, and gone to become a clerk in a tea merchant's office in London.

Presumably his father had cut him off without a shilling and there was no account of any inheritance in Cyril Savage's family archives. Grandfather Johnson had never got on with his sister Melody either.

Cyril Savage had met his Aunt Melody once when he was a child. She had been in London on business and had called on his father and mother, her sole remaining relatives. She hadn't taken on Cyril at all, nor he to her. And she had disapproved of the rest of the family, too; Cyril's sister, since dead, and his brother, who had later gone down-hill to the dogs. Miss Johnson had been too starchy and exacting altogether the visit had been a failure and she had said farewell and departed for good. The family had broken up later and Aunt Melody had grown into a distant memory, a sort of ghost from the past.

Cyril was a bank cashier in London and was keen on money. He had made several attempts to re-establish contact with his great-aunt, with an eye to ingratiating himself with her. After all, the Johnsons had been reputed to be very comfortably off. They had owned a very profitable mine in Plumpton Bois when the lodes were flourishing. His mother's great-grandfather had, he knew, started a mine of his own, raised himself from a modest miner to a local bigwig, built *Johnsons Place*, and moved to it from a two-up and two-down cottage. But all Cyril's approaches to his aunt had been repulsed. She had snubbed him, never answered his letters or his persistent Christmas cards.

Once only, when he had written to say that he would be in the vicinity on holidays and would call on her, had she sent him a formal note. 'Miss Johnson is unwell and is unable to receive visitors.' After that, he'd given up.

And now, like a bolt from the blue, the legacy. A house and its contents. And what a house! Large, damp, rambling and shabby.

When Mr. Jeremiah Cunliffe, his aunt's lawyer in Povington, had written to him and explained that Miss Johnson wished the house and all its contents to pass to her sole surviving relative,

Cyril Savage had pictured a fine patrician place. He was due to retire from the bank in four years and maybe he could then settle there, his mother's family home. But now ... Not on your life ...

'You'd better call and see the place and then come back to me and let me know what you decide to do about it,' Mr. Cunliffe had told him when Savage had called on his way to inspect his windfall. 'You may find it somewhat neglected. Of late years your aunt has not been at all well and unable to manage her affairs properly. Had I not done my modest share of keeping an eye on things, they might have been far worse ...'

Mr. Savage had grown bold.

'Who inherits the money, if I'm only to get the property?'

Mr. Cunliffe was a small, aged, wiry man with close-cut sandy hair, sandy eyebrows and a benevolent expression for the occasion. His benevolence turned to acid at the question.

'There was very little left. A few hundred pounds in the bank. No investments and, as far as I can ascertain, no property elsewhere. You are the only one to receive any substantial benefit.'

'Who gets the bank balance?'

Mr. Savage was a persistent man. Mr. Cunliffe regarded him bellicosely over his spectacles.

'I do. She and I had been friends for more than sixty years and during that time, I helped her with all her financial affairs. After her legacy to you, she left me the residue. It was in the nature of a mere honorarium, for I collected very little from her in the way of fees during her lifetime. Are you satisfied, or shall I read the will to you? It is quite short.'

Mr. Savage decided that he'd been swindled by a sharp lawyer and that it was no use arguing about it.

'You needn't bother. I see your point.'

'The house and grounds of *Johnsons Place* have been neglected of late. Miss Johnson's maid, a woman of over seventy, who'd been with her since she was a girl taken from an orphanage, and nursed your aunt through her last illness, left about a week ago. I would have urged her to stay until you took over, but she had made other arrangements. So, as I couldn't find a suitable caretaker in the vicinity, I had to leave things. A neighbour is keeping an eye on the place, however. I'm sorry, but I did my best. You see, Plumpton Bois was, until quite recently, an almost deserted village. There are very few domestic workers there, if any. The owners of the properties are either elderly retired people, or else residents from nearby towns who come and go over weekends ...'

Mr. Savage had left the lawyer feeling very unhappy and dissatisfied. He had a presentiment that somewhere, something was wrong ...

The whole interview came back to him as he stood before the door of the room on the left of the tiled passage. He turned the knob, but the door didn't move. He put his knee to it and irritably banged it open. When he stepped inside, he recoiled.

This was what must have been a ceremonial sitting-room. It smelled of damp horsehair and decayed curtains. There were stiff little chairs, a brass fender before the fireplace and a skin hearthrug which looked to be suffering from ringworm. A small Sheraton desk in one corner was the only article of furniture worth looking at. The walls and mantelpiece were littered with framed and fading photographs of the Johnson family. Mr. Savage recoiled from none of these, but from the state of the room.

A large mahogany chiffonier had all its drawers out and had been resolutely rummaged. The desk had suffered the same indignity and its locks had been forced. As though seeking a hiding place under the floor, the intruder had partly rolled back the carpet, a worn green affair, and apparently examined the boards under it. He had even been up the chimney, for there were marks of soot here and there in the room, as though he hadn't minded his dirty hands or gloves.

This was the last straw for Mr. Savage. He made whimpering noises as he paused to recover from the shock and then, ignoring his wife, rushed from room to room, upstairs and down. Without exception, they had suffered a similar going-over, but order had apparently been somewhat restored there. As though the searcher — whoever he was — had originally tried to make a neat job, but that his time had run out as he progressed.

The mattresses and feather beds in the two furnished bedrooms had been opened and plumbed and there were feathers scattered all over the place like relics of a destructive fox in a poultry yard.

Cyril Savage was almost hysterical with rage and confusion until intense hatred of the unknown intruder steadied him. Meanwhile, his wife, infected by the crazy atmosphere created by her husband, had collapsed in an armchair in the dining-room, Miss Johnson's living place, with a round oak table, straw bottomed chairs and a large Welsh dresser with its drawers gaping wide.

Savage didn't even bother about his wife. He continued to rush here and there, like a caged rat seeking an outlet. Upstairs and down, to the attics and back. He was not a courageous man, but very impulsive. That was the reason he hadn't got very far in the bank. He'd made a lot of stupid mistakes during his career, charging like a bull at a gate when faced by a problem. He would have killed the wrecker of his aunt's house had he found him. That would have been another mistake.

Finally, the only place he found unexplored was the cavity under the stairs, close by a large door, which presumably gave access to the cellars. When Savage tried to open it he found it locked. There was no key. He sought everywhere for it, his anger re-kindled. He was a sorry sight. His face streaked with soot, his eyes staring, his lips twisted in a mirthless grin. He still wore his cap and raincoat; the former askew over one eye, the latter stained with dust, oil and soot picked up during his wild search. He could not find the key anywhere. He put his shoulder to the obstinate door, but it resisted him. He kicked it, but it did not move.

At last, in a transport of rage, he took up a heavy hall chair and smashed at the lock. The door opened suddenly from the weight of the blow.

Mr. Savage paused as though surprised at what he had accomplished. He felt the clammy tainted air ooze from the black yawning cavity and surround him, rancid and full of decay. That was all.

When Mrs. Savage came-to a little later, she sat upright and listened. Not a sound indoors. She screamed her husband's name which echoed round the empty house. There was no reply. She slowly made her way to the hall, gripping the furniture to hold her up and give her some confidence.

She found her husband dead at the top of the cellar steps from a fearful blow on the head. She gave a great moan and, in a burst of terrified strength, ran screaming from the place.